COMMENTARY

I did enjoy reading *Adrift*, but what really struck me were the relationships that the two main characters had with the homeless and the runaway they were "serving."

Seeing God move the hearts and minds of those who are vulnerable, hurting, and have experienced trauma as all of our homeless men, women and children have—this is the reason we do what we do. When we are able to show them respect, treat them with dignity, and let them know that they matter to us and to God, this begins what will be the healing process for many.

Sonny Pyon, San Diego Rescue Mission

Adrift is a "can't put it down" book. You will see what transformations can happen in the lives of the homeless. I always tell my team of twenty volunteers that we can win them to Christ one at a time, and as you see in this story, it works. We need to sow our time into their lives and teach them they can overcome. For forty six years the Gleaning Fields Foundation has brought physical and spiritual help to those in need. *Adrift* is not just for those in ministry, but all who fear the homeless should read and see what God's love can do when we reach out and follow our hearts in His name.

Rosa Davis, Gleaning Fields Foundation, Vista CA
www.gleaningfield.com

I found John Pascal's *Adrift* a wonderful mix of warm and tender, troubled, distressed and memorable characters from the world of the homeless and those who care for them by offering the promise of salvation and true peace.

William Lynes, MD—Author of "A Surgeon's Knot"

Adrift is classified as a work of fiction, however, it provides its readers with a real life experience. John Pascal artfully draws us in to relate to well-depicted characters who reveal how challenging it is to be a compassionate Christian in our times. The realistic boots-on-the ground situations are gut wrenching at times, but a dynamic of saving grace runs through this story like a living stream. Pascal helps the reader re-arrange their relationship with God by moments of connection, as does the unquestionable presence of the "least of the least" among us who may become our spiritual guides.

The MacCanon Brown Homeless Shelter is led by a woman who has been a community leader, public speaker and advocate for the homeless and marginalized for 28 years. It serves Wisconsin's most impoverished area with transformational solidarity in what was once a warehouse. Now it is a citywide Help Center in Milwaukee.

Sister MacCanon Brown (SFCC)

Those who are born into a new spirit with Jesus Christ are the bearers of good news and tender caretakers for those in need. The blessings and the hand of God can lead one toward rich encounters, miraculous opportunities and a new vision of hope.

I recommend this refreshing novel. It centers in on the heart-wrenching concern for the lost and distressed, and motivates us to love each other tenderly. I should also mention that, weaving through this story, a wonderful romance unfolds.

Sarah McCrudden, author of "The Catholic Omission."

God has a special place in His heart for the most marginalized and hurting. Personally, the greatest transformations I have witnessed in fifty years of ministry have come from the homeless community. The great joy of Christian ministry is to witness a person discovering that God is real and watch the transformation in their life. In *Adrift,* John Pascal offers a perfect picture of the results that can be attained when God's love captures the hearts of those who are willing to be His hands and care for the less fortunate.

Roger Friend, Pastor: Vista Christian Fellowship, Vista California

Also by John Pascal:

The Bee

Domes

2248 (These three are *The Revelation Trilogy)*

Prisoner 1171

Wingin' It

My Child

Fatherless

Truth Wars

Jesus said, "Love your neighbor
as yourself." Luke, 10:27

ONE

The labels on the little water bottles read "Jesus loves you." Brad McKinley stuffed two of them he hadn't given out into his back pack as he hurried into the ER. Three EMTs were outside unloading a man from their ambulance onto a gurney and the sound of an approaching siren signaled another patient was on his way.

Brad slipped in ahead of the team and approached an elderly man in a wheelchair who sat blocking the entrance. He grabbed the handles pulled him back. "Sorry, Gramps. Gotta make way for some incoming."

The man looked up at him, his head shaking side to side. "Wait a minute." He pointed to a woman behind the registration desk. "That girl said my son was picking me up here."

Brad grinned at her. "And if Sally said so, you can count on it." She narrowed her eyes and returned a pained smile. "But, please wait here away from the doors."

The old guy peered at the bulging pack on Brad's back. "Yeah, and who are you, Fella?"

"I'm a physician's assistant—just coming in for my shift."
He patted the man's arm. "And I better go see if these guys need any
help."

The gurney wheeled past. Brad winced at the sight of the
black man's face, contorted in pain, his blue shirt covered in blood.
He caught a whiff of gun powder as a nurse and another PA waved
for the paramedics to follow them.

Brad walked over to Sally's counter. "Do you know where
this shooting happened?"

She looked at her computer screen. "Downtown--that
'mostly peaceful' protest."

"Uh, oh, you'll have a hundred reporters swarming your desk
any minute now."

She shook her dark curls. "Nah. Probably just local TV."

"Really? Why do you say that?"

She looked him squarely in the eye. "Cause he's a
policeman, not a protester. Say, you better get changed. They might
need extra help in the OR."

Brad rolled his eyes and scooted down the stairs to the locker
room.

"Well, look who's almost on time. What a surprise."

Brad grimaced at his friend Don's greeting and pulled off his
back pack. "I think I'm *early*."

"Only missed 'early' by two minutes, but who's counting?"
Don pointed to a clock on the wall and straightened his white coat in

the locker room mirror. "Look, our internship is almost over. You want to get hired or not?"

Brad began to pull on his uniform in haste. "Of course I do. I start out early, but sometimes I get waylaid along the way."

"Oh, yeah? But if you took the *bus* you'd be on time, right, Buddy?"

"You know my apartments only a few blocks away."

Don inhaled an exaggerated sniff. "My *point* is you wouldn't come in late reeking of marijuana after walking by that creep nest down the street."

"They're not creeps, just homeless, but I admit I enjoy talking with those guys. I tell them about Jesus and drop a few bucks on them most mornings. So what?"

"I'll tell you what." Don pointed at his feet and shuddered. "Look, you're wearing *sandals*. What if you step on one of their needles, huh?"

"I put those in the city's used needle box."

Don gave a wry chuckle. "And I suppose you carry a plastic bag for poops too." He stood in front of Brad and made eye contact. "Look, Brad, I know your dad is some kind of a do-good pastor, but you only pick up needles if a doctor drops one, okay?"

"You worry too much, Don." Brad gave himself a quick shot of spray deodorant, whisked a comb through his light brown hair and slammed his locker. "Where are you assigned today?"

"I'm working the ER for the rest of the week, you?"

"Fourth floor, General Medicine, but I was in the ER two weeks ago." He sucked in a breath. "That's when this guy Willie came in. He almost died of an overdose."

The intercom blared: "Mister Donald Skepstrom, report to the emergency room stat."

"Aw, chees. Gotta go." Don hurried toward the door but he turned back with a scowl. "Don't tell me. This 'Willie' lives on the street nearby, right?"

"Not exactly. He lives in an *alley* next to the street two blocks away and he told me this morning he thinks the methadone treatment must be working cause he feels so lousy."

Don shook his head and raised a finger. "Hey, don't forget-- this Friday night at Murphy's. My wife is bringing her cousin and you promised to meet her. I've only seen her picture, but she's gorgeous."

"So that's why Melissa never introduced you, huh?

"Very funny. It's at seven. Don't be your usual late self."

Brad pursed his lips. "Oh, wait, I think I'm counseling Willie that night."

Don swung into the hallway and spoke with his back turned. "Not funny."

*   *   *

After his long day at work, Brad picked up two macho burritos across the street from the hospital, stuffed the bag into his backpack and headed home. He thought, *What created the situation that made so many homeless? Some ridicule them as lazy, others say they're all on drugs or just crazy people with no where to go. We've got nine million people in this city and our politicians keep saying more money will "solve" the problem. It's just getting worse.*

Coming up on "Willie's alley," the urine smell seemed stronger than usual. New tents now dotted the sidewalk, some emanating moans. A man screamed from somewhere down the alley. He craned his neck, but couldn't see where it came from. *Wonder if I can help.*

A bearded old man he'd never seen before sat against the wall of the building near the alley entrance clinking a metal bowl next to him. Rheumy eyes looked up into his. Brad smiled, dropped in a few dollars and a "God bless you" before he began a few tentative steps down the alley.

Half way down he passed a man with long unkempt hair wearing dirty pajamas. He was swaying back and forth repeating, "Don't hit your neighbor—hit your neighbor—bad, bad." Brad shook his head and moved on. *This one's off his meds.*

Willie sat on a wooden box beside his little tent watching his approach, a passive look on his face. His beard was starting to grow back, but the hospital had washed his tattered jeans and he'd

11

acquired a Hawaiian shirt from somewhere. Brad gave him a wave. "Hi, Willie, it's me again. Who's been screaming?"

He pointed at pajama man. "That one shouts when he feels like it."

"I get it. So, how're *you* doing?"

Willie shrugged and gave him a "whatever" gesture with one hand.

"Okay if I talk with you awhile?"

Willie's eyes narrowed. "Okay, but if it's that Jesus thing again, I've heard it before. Doc."

"Nah, I'll save that for another time." Brad grinned. "Still off the nasties, I hope?"

"Yeah." He sighed. "But that methadone doesn't charge your batteries, and I'm feeling like a rag in the trash."

"Well, I'm glad you're hanging tough. Give it some time." Brad slipped off his back pack and pulled out a white bag and a water bottle. "Care for a burrito?"

That perked him up. Willie returned a brief smile. "Hey, thanks, man. What's that clear stuff you got? Some sauce?"

Brad squirted some on his hands and rubbed them together. "I like to wash up before eating." He handed it to Willie and gestured for him to use it.

"Like soap?"

"Sort of, but no water needed. Can I ask you about yourself? You never told me your story."

"You mean, so you can tell me about how perfect *you* are compared to me."

Brad laughed. "Perfect? Hardly. Meet 'Mister Mistakes.' Flunked out of high school once and I've been dropped by no less than two girlfriends in the past year."

"Yeah?" He frowned—a look of skepticism on his face. "Well, how'd you get a job at the hospital?"

Brad spied a syringe on the concrete nearby. He took out a plastic bag from his pack and deftly scooped it inside without touching the needle. "My dad turned me around. I hated him at first, but he laid on what they call 'tough love.' He finally got through to me, but the most important turnaround was finding Jesus. Wait, I know you don't want to hear that story right now."

Willie munched quietly on his burrito and stared at his toes. He mumbled quietly. "Me? I made it halfway through college before dad died with a mountain of debt. Mom married someone else—moved to Denver. Haven't talked to her in years."

"No kidding, Willie—*college*? What was your major?"

"Computer science and even though I couldn't stay in school, I almost got my degree on line. I was living with a friend, but he got busted for selling meth." He looked around and opened up his hands. "He went to jail and I bounced onto the street."

"And I guess he sold you some too, right?"

"Sure. I sold a lot of it. Had to get money for the opioids."

"Still selling?"

"I ain't saying."

Brad chuckled. "And I ain't telling, but hey, you're off the hard stuff now. Maybe you could finish your degree."

Willie pulled his knees up to his chest and rested his head on them. "Look, you're a nice guy but I don't want to talk about this no more."

"Okay." Brad looked at Willie's red and swollen bare feet. "What's your shoe size?"

"Ten. Why?"

Brad slipped his sandals off and strapped them on Willie's feet. "They told me I need to start wearing real shoes at the hospital." Willie's mouth dropped open, an incredulous look on his face.

Brad hefted his back pack over his shoulders. "Well, see you later, friend."

Willie silently stared at his footwear. A large tear rolled down his cheek.

TWO

Murphy's Bar was humming with music, people and smoke. Don nursed his second rum and coke while his wife, Melissa, chatted with her friend, an attractive redhead poured into a tight green dress. Even separated by one stool, Don felt himself gagging on her cloud of perfume.

He interrupted them. ""Uh, I should say something about Brad."

She returned a demure smile as he went on. "Not sure what Melissa told you about him. He's a bit awkward around women, but he has a good heart. Right now he's helping the homeless."

"Oh, I think shy men are sweet." She did a happy little shudder. "And a philanthropist, too? I just adore those big fund raising parties. You know, once I got a man to donate a thousand dollars to charity for just one dance with me."

Melissa raised a finger. "Uh, that's not exactly…"

Don spied Brad coming over, stood up and waved at him. "Hey, Buddy, there you are. I was worried you might be a no show."

Don gestured to the ladies. "You know Melissa. This is Judy." He motioned to his friend. "Judy: Brad."

When Brad took her hand, Melissa shook her head. "She goes by *Juniah* now. Don forgot."

Brad muttered, "So sorry I'm late, Jun-ya."

Juniah added a little finger massage to the handshake before she released him and held up her Martini glass with a radiant smile. "It's jew-nigh-yah. Pleased ta meetcha. I'll call you Bradey, okay?"

"Uh, anything you like, Juniah. A hospital case ran a bit long--my apologies."

"Well, Doctor Bradey, don't worry. Pull up a stool and order a relaxer."

As Brad sat down between Don and Juniah, Don tapped him on the shoulder. "Melissa said she couldn't believe you were still unmarried. Should I tell her why?"

Melissa leaned forward and gave her husband an evil look. Don grinned. "Only kidding."

Juniah leaned in close to Brad, looked up at him and purred: "So, Bradey, tell me about all those other doctors you work with. Do you consult for them?"

"Uh, I…"

The bartender stood in front of him. "What's your pleasure?"

"I'll have a small house Shiraz."

"Ah, see." Juniah smiled. "I could tell you were the conservative type, Doctor Brady. I'm psychic, you know."

"Well, ahem, I guess I've never been much of a drinker."

Juniah glanced over her shoulder at Melissa. "And this type of a man is, like you said, a real steady Eddie. You did good, Missy."

She swiveled back to Brad, brushed her leg against his and put a wiggly-fingered hand on his shoulder. Dons eyebrows shot up. "Tell me, Bradey, what do you do for fun when you can tear yourself away from all those patients?"

"Well, I like golf, reading, going to plays, and sometimes I go fishing with a friend. He owns a small yacht and we go sailing down the coast."

"Ohhh," Juniah squeezed his arm and moved her face close to his. "I just *adore* yachts."

Don gave his wife a thumbs up but her furrowed brow puzzled him.

"Well, say," Brad grinned. "I'm sure Jimmy wouldn't mind if you came along for a day trip. You'd have to get up really early, though."

"Oooh, count me in," Juniah bubbled. "I'm already shopping in my mind for what to wear."

Brad shrugged. "That's easy—a sweatshirt, shorts and sunscreen." The bartender placed his wine goblet down but Brad's eyes never left Juniah. "Have you done much fishing?"

"No, silly." She giggled. "That's for you. I'll be laying out on the deck in a new swimsuit and sipping drinks."

Brad laughed. "That'll be real distracting. Maybe I won't be doing much fishing either."

Don was getting worried about his wife's reaction. Melissa pushed her drink aside. Her brow furrows had doubled in size, and she stared at the ceiling.

"But you didn't tell me, sweetie…" Juniah cocked her head to one side and pursed her lips. "No, wait. Let me guess." She downed the rest of her martini in one gulp and squinted her eyes. "*Neurology,* that's my guess. Is that your specialty?"

"No wait. I'm not a doctor," Brad blurted. "I'm training to be a physician assistant—same as Don. Didn't Melissa tell you?"

Juniah's jaw dropped. She stiffened upright, and swiveled to face Melissa with a look of horror. "You told me he worked with the other doctors at the hospital."

"I never said *other* doctors." Melissa scowled in annoyance. "I said he works *with* doctors at the hospital and he's Don's friend."

The horror was morphing into anger. "You did *to* say 'other'."

"Did not—look Brad's the nicest guy, like ever. I had no idea you'd feel…"

Juniah stood up and turned to Brad. Her word temperature dropped down to thirty two degrees. "It was nice to meet you Brad, but I forgot. I have to be somewhere right now." She turned and walked away.

Brad stood up and spoke to her disappearing form. "Nice to meet you too. Can I call you about fishing?"

When he turned back, Melissa gave him a hug. "Look, Brad, I'm just so sorry. I knew she was a little that way, but you didn't deserve this."

"That's okay. I'm used to it."

Don gave him a grin and clapped his hand on his shoulder. "Anyway, man, dinner's on us and the good news is there's a pool table in the next room."

THREE

Saving Grace Church used to have a small Christian school attached but when it grew in size, they joined a larger school nearby. Now the facility has become a women's shelter.

Martha Eldridge, the shelter's manager, stood up behind her desk at the sound of screeches and commotion down the hall. *Hope no one's hurt.* She pushed back some stray gray hairs from her bun and quick-stepped down the corridor toward the noise. *No, it's laughter.*

At the doorway to their art room, Martha watched Jackie, one of her volunteers, holding a twisted balloon animal while a group of women gathered around her giggling.   Feigning a stern policeman's voice, Martha barked, "Okay, what's going on in here?"

Jackie twirled around, blonde pigtail flailing, hiding the balloons behind her back. One woman hollered "Busted!" and all the students screeched with laughter.

Jackie stood in front of their balloon creation, cocked her head to one side and displayed a look of pure innocence. "Nothing, Mrs. Eldridge."

One of the students was laughing so hard, her head fell to the work table as she pounded it with a fist.

Martha stifled a grin but spoke with demure perfection. "Jackie, please come by my office when you are finished with this class."

"Yes, ma'am."

Martha pretended to strain her neck to see what was being hidden. "We need to talk."

The students whispered, "Ooooh," and laughed again.

Martha gave Jackie a smile when she knocked on the doorframe. A large black dog came up to her, wagging its tail and Jackie rewarded him with a scratch behind the ears.

"That's 'Keeper.'" Martha said. "She's a shelter rescue I've been training at home to be a therapy dog. See, we thought she was a keeper so we decided to keep her."

"I get it. The ladies will love her. Look, if this is about that video shoot last weekend, I apologize. I had no idea you were going to use it in a promotional ad or I would have worked on another angle. I just thought it would be fun to *pretend* to be doing streachies and Jazzercise and make a parody of it. The ladies had a good time."

"No, no, Jackie. We *loved* it. That skit will live on as a classic in the archives of Saving Grace Homeless Shelter. Have a seat."

"Uh, oh." She bit her lip. "You found out about the balloon, right?"

Jackie was still standing. Martha laughed and gestured toward a chair. "Jackie, you probably have no idea what a delight you are. We'll miss you terribly when you go back to college this fall."

"I can come back for some weekends and vacations, but what did you want to talk to me about?"

"I'll tell you in a moment but now, since you insist, I guess I better hear the balloon story."

Jackie sat down and Keepher's head quickly found a lap to rest on. "Do I *have* to?"

"Oh, yes. I've just been treated to a roomful of homeless and abused women laughing like they were at a frat party, and I *love* God's miracles, so yes. Please tell me."

"Hardly miraculous." Jackie blew out through her cheeks. "My daddy makes the balloon animals for kids at county fairs and such, and he taught me so I could entertain the children at our church picnics. Now I *know* I'm supposed to be teaching an art class, but this is kind of like sculpture, right?"

"And the laughter?"

"Ann Malory made a funny looking gorilla and we were laughing at it."

Martha cocked her head to one side with a quizzical look. "Something tells me there's more to it than that, Jackie."

22

"Oh, all right." She looked up at the ceiling and shook her ponytail side to side. "The gorilla has a pee-pee. She made a mistake twisting it together."

Martha pouted. "I *see*, and what did you do about this anatomical correctness?"

"Well I was going to show them how to tie it off and puncture it without deflating Mister Kong—that's what they named him, but some ladies were screaming in protest."

Martha couldn't hold back a grin. "So?"

"So, we put it to a vote—seven to four against mutilation." Jackie produced a gigantic smile.

"Tell me this Kong Man won't be displayed."

"Yes and no. He's being moved to the closet where the sewing machines are. Tomorrow he'll get a pair of custom made swim trunks."

"Oh, good." Martha breathed a sigh of relief. She leaned back in her chair and lowered her voice. "Now I want to talk to you about another matter."

Jackie's eyes widened. "Yes, ma'am?"

"You have a God given talent for cheering people up--for giving them hope. I'd like you to consider taking on a major challenge--Gina Giannopoulos. She's clinically depressed, withdrawn and has been suicidal. She sits in our garden most days staring straight ahead, won't talk to anyone and barely eats her dinner when she comes in for the night. I'm really worried about her."

"I've seen her. But I never realized…"

"I'd like you to consider spending some time with her."

"Me? But I don't have any training in social work, medicine or psychology. I'm an art major."

"True, but you have something better than education. You have a spiritual anointing to do the Lord's work. Remember your grandfather? You told me he was an African missionary but he didn't finish high school."

Jackie's hand covered her mouth. "I just don't know."

"I'm not saying it will be easy, but even if you fail, it's still better than never trying. I just hope she won't take away that wonderful smile of yours."

FOUR

Jackie hoisted her art materials under her right arm so she could open the latch to the garden gate. The sign on it read, "Private Property. No Camping. Guests of Saving Grace Church only."

Two women were chatting in the rectangular lawn area. Others were stretched out on towels to enjoy the sun and one squatted under an oak tree, nursing an infant. The women weren't allowed into the church meeting hall until five o'clock when they would claim a bed for the night and plunk their belongings on it. Early arrivals, however, could wait in their side yard garden.

Jackie looked forward to the six o'clock fellowship with them and a meal, but even more to the chapel service that followed. After that the homeless women were free to just relax, read or choose an educational program in the evening. The Church offered Bible Study, computer basics, remedial English, Survival Economics, sewing, and an art class.

Jackie schlepped her load to the far corner where a woman in a gray dress sat slumped on a bench, staring off into space. *That must be Gina,* she thought. Her quarry in sight, she began setting up her easel in front of the iron bench. "Hello," She said in her cheeriest voice. No response.

"Hope you won't mind if I sit next to you and do a little painting."

No response—well, maybe a grunt.

Jackie shrugged and began to draw. In a few moments the shape of the queen palm opposite them emerged from charcoal strokes on the canvas. From the corner of her eye, Jackie saw the woman making furtive glances at her work.

The artist began to add a background of shrubs and a distant ocean under a cloud filled blue sky. She hummed a happy tune. The woman humphed, slouched and turned away but she continued to hum.

Jackie took her time with the trunk, merging it into the shape of a ballerina. Each graceful leaf was wafted by an imaginary breeze. Her companion wrestled into different positions settling for hands under chin and elbows on knees. She closed her eyes except for the quick peeks she couldn't resist. When a bird appeared in the canvas sky the woman finally spoke. "There's only a brick wall behind that tree."

Jackie thought: *At last, she speaks.* She gave her a grin sweet enough to make sawdust tasty. "I know, but I wanted the right background to show how graceful the palm fronds are in the wind. With a little imagination you can see the sky beyond those confining walls."

"Is that supposed to be a person in the trunk? It's just a *tree*, Missy."

"Yes, but imagine the tree as though it *was* a person. I see a ballerina balancing on one foot, about to pirouette with arms becoming palm fronds. See how I turned the leaf tips so they look like graceful fingers."

The woman stood up. "A tree is a tree, you twit."

"But, use your imagination. If you were to *pretend* it's a person. What would you see?"

"Humph, cernuous fronds—she's despondent."

Jackie's eyes widened at the big words. "But, what's she doing?"

The woman squinted at the painting, turned away and headed for the gate. Suddenly, she swiveled around, snarling at Jackie. "She's a woman on a tight rope and she's about to fall off."

FIVE

Brad shook his head as he passed by piles of human waste in a tree planter. *Whoa, why have they stopped using...*He glanced across the street. *They're gone—the porta-potties are gone. Why?*

The rheumy-eyed old man now sat in a rocking chair at the entrance to the alley. He was whistling "Daisy, Daisy" as he rocked. Brad dropped a couple of dollars in his pan and said hello.

"Bless you, lad."

"Say, what happened to the two porta-potties that Christ Church had in their yard across the street?"

"The city made them take 'em out. The locals complained it didn't look good to see them—somethin' like that."

Brad pointed to the tree planter. "So they think that looks better, huh?"

"A cop told me the pastor was the only one who stood up at the council meeting. He said the city just wanted them gone 'cause it showed everyone they'd failed."

"Really." Brad threw his head back and shook it side to side. "So no one cares about public health? I think I'll talk to some people at the hospital. Maybe we can at least get one put up down the alley."

"That'd be real sweet of you, lad."

Brad gave him a thumbs-up and headed down the alley. Walking carefully to avoid needles, he looked around for Willie, but his tent flap was open and he was gone. Farther down, the man wearing the dirty pajamas, sat against the wall. He swayed forward and back crying out over and over: "They're bad—they're bad. They're coming now. They're coming for us."

Opposite Willie's place a young black man sat on a stool strumming a ukulele. A few strips of brown paint clung to its bare white wood revealing its original color. "George, any idea where Willie is?"

"He said he wasn't feeling well again and staggered off. I thought he was just gonna go puke somewhere, but he ain't been back for a couple of hours."

"Huh, well, I'm on my way to the hospital. Maybe he went to the ER."

"Maybe. Hope he's okay."

Brad handed him a couple of dollars. "Me too. Here, keep an eye on his stuff, okay?"

"Sure." George returned a large, white grin. "I always do, but thanks."

Brad quickened his pace toward the hospital. *Willie's liver enzymes were high and his kidneys were less than perfect. Maybe they let him go too soon.*

SIX

Brad changed into his uniform, went directly to the emergency room and approached the registrar. "Sally, did a man come through here about two hours ago named Willie?"

Sally stuck a pink fingernail between her teeth and checked her register. "Uh, there was a William Clark. Maybe that's him. He staggered in and fainted."

"Admitted?"

"Uh, huh. He's on 2B, room 120."

"Admitting diagnosis?"

Sally checked her record sheet and shrugged. "It just says, 'evaluation, syncope'. Doctor Gordon was assigned and your friend Don went up with him."

Brad knocked on the doorframe of room 120 and walked in. Willie looked at him with faintly yellow eyes and a weak smile. "Hey, Doc."

"Hi, Willie. Lemme guess: hepatitis B."

"Good guess. That's what Doctor Gordon thinks, but he's runnin' tests. I sure feel punk, though."

Brad moved in closer, squinted his eyes and looked at Willie's arm. "You been using someone else's needles?"

"Nah," he shook his head. "I'm clean—honest. And even before rehab, I always rinsed them off first."

"News flash, Pal. That doesn't sterilize them." He grinned. "But I'm glad you're off the hard stuff. I've been worrying about you."

"Thanks, doc. That means a lot. This hep thing—can it kill me?"

"Nah," He spread his arms out. "Assuming that's all it is, we have good treatments."

Willie relaxed back against the pillows and looked at the ceiling. "Bring 'em on. I feel like crap."

"Anything I can do for you?"

Willie looked up. "Yeah. Could you bring me the black back pack in my tent?"

"Should I pass it by our drug-sniffing German Shepherd first?"

Willie chuckled. "No need, and I'm not dealing neither."

"Okay, I'll try and swing by there on my lunch time. Right now I have to get to work on my floor."

"Thanks, man."

Brad pointed a finger at him. "Willie, do you believe God can heal people?"

Willie squirmed about for a moment. "I guess--if there is a God, He can do anything He wants."

"There is, and He gives believers His authority, too. Mind if I say a prayer for you?"

Willie tossed up his hands. "Knock yourself out."

Brad placed his hand on Willie's forehead. "Lord, I believe you want to fully restore Willie--in body, mind and spirit. I ask You for mercy and I pray right now for Willie's healing. Amen."

"Oh, good." With a quizzical look, "Does that mean I can leave now?"

"Maybe, but lets humor the doctors for awhile longer." He walked to the door, but looked back. "I'll check back after my shift."

"Okay with me. I like sleeping in this bed."

As Brad turned to leave, a nurse's aid stood in the doorway. She scowled and shook her finger at him. He gave her a puzzled look, shrugged his shoulders and left.

He wondered if the woman didn't like his prayer—yeah, it wasn't much like the way his dad prayed.

Brad spied Dr Gordon at the nurse's station. "Hi. William Clark was my patient a few months ago with an overdose. Did he come in with hepatitis this time?"

Gordon nodded. "His hepatic enzymes are above the readout range and he has bile in his urine. We're waiting on the viral type and X-rays but hepatitis seems certain."

Brad opened his hands. "But it's acute and you caught it early so the prognosis should be hopeful, right?"

Gordon looked up from the chart. "Unfortunately, no. We started Viread and interferon, but Mister Clark's lifestyle damaged his liver. Look at his chart from the past admission. Alcohol and drugs did their dirty work over the years, and this infection put him on a downward spiral."

"Do you think it will be fatal?"

"I'd say so—maybe a few weeks, but certainly in a couple of months."

Brad grimaced. *So prayer is all that's left.*

SEVEN

Jackie arrived at the shelter earlier in the afternoon than usual. It was drizzling lightly and the garden was deserted. She carried her easel and art box under one arm and a beach umbrella under the other as she struggled to open the gate.

I love the way it smells when it's raining, she thought, and made her way to the bench in the far corner and put her box on it.

Once the stand was screwed into the ground, the large umbrella covered the bench and her easel. She patted out a dry spot on the bench with a towel from her box, and sat.

As she waited for inspiration, two fat ground squirrels popped out of the far fence. She thought they were playing some game with their run—freeze—run motions. Jackie giggled at their tail-in-the-air antics, and began to draw.

She had just begun to paint color over her charcoal sketch when her scowling assignment slouched in and trudged toward her. The woman pointed to the bench. "Mind?" she said.

Jackie whisked her towel over the spot. "Course not." She grinned at her, trying unsuccessfully to make eye contact. "I'm Jackie, by the way. Sorry to see your shoulders looking cernuous today."

The woman sat staring straight ahead and grunted, "Gina." A hint of a smile flickered over her face and she turned to Jackie. "So you looked up that word, did you?"

"I did. Cool word. I'm gonna use it." Jackie thought *Wow, she's talking to me.* "Your sweater looks soaked, Gina. Here, hang it up on a spoke inside the umbrella. It should dry a little."

She complied, wrung it out and wedged it between the fabric and a spoke. Jackie slipped off her own jacket and draped it over Gina's shivering shoulders. She returned a look of surprise.

The women lapsed into silence and Jackie resumed painting.

The squirrels had run away when Gina came in, but now they darted out and began to eat the flowers at the base of the palm tree. Jackie whispered, "Ah, there you are." She squinted over her canvas. "And now I see the shape of your scruffy little tails."

From the corner of her eye, Jackie watched Gina beginning to squirm around and peek at her work. Finally, Gina came out with, "You're painting *vermin?*"

Jackie giggled. "I know everyone sees these rats as pests but I think they're interesting art subjects—especially those big, fat ones."

"They're marmots, not rats, and they probably live in that open space behind us."

"Really?" Now there was eye contact. "Gosh, I didn't know that."

35

"Tree squirrels aren't from the marmot tribe, but these ground squirrels are. Still, they're all vermin." She sighed. "It's cold out here. Think I'll wait on the porch 'til it's time."

"Sure, I understand." She pointed at her art subjects. "What I got out of watching these little guys is their instinct for cooperation. One is a lookout and chirping at danger while the others munch on our flowers."

"Men either shoot them, trap them or poison them—and for good reason."

"I know, but I really think God has a purpose for every creature he created, and every one of us, too."

Gina's face was sullen, but Jackie persisted, "Before you go, ell me what *you* see when you look at them?"

Gina slipped the jacket off, took her sweater down from the umbrella, and headed down the exit path. Jackie thought she wasn't going to answer, but suddenly, she turned toward the squirrels, raised her arms and shouted, "I see *fear*." They scattered.

EIGHT

Brad stood on a hospital balcony talking to his dad. "Dad, I'm on a short break. Can I ask your help with something?"

"Of course. What's the problem?"

"It's about a patient—one who's not doing so well."

He chuckled. "You know a lot more about medicine than I do, son."

"It's not about medicine, its…" Two nurses came out with coffee cups and sat at a table. Brad moved to the edge of the balcony and turned away for privacy. "Dad, you remember Evelyn Holt, the black lady whose cancer went away?"

"Forget any of God's miracles? Course not. They gave her three months to live and now she's running our Sunday School."

"Right. I want to pray that same prayer you used for my patient."

"Ah, ha." Dad sighed. "Now I understand. Son, just reciting words does not produce healing. God wants us to pray with authority and belief. Still, miraculous healings are uncommon."

"Authority, huh." Brad blew out through his cheeks, grasped the handrail and searched the distant hills. "I don't think I'm certified."

"You're born again, Son. You have more power than you realize. Besides that, I think God's favor is more likely to go with the young and the passionate, especially those who are just beginning a mission."

"Don't know about a mission, but I'd sure like to help this guy."

"Has your patient accepted Jesus?"

"He's been resistant."

"Being faced with death often changes minds. I know you know how to lead him in a salvation prayer. Save his soul first."

"Brad was chuckling. "I get it, Dad. First things first. Then what?"

"Then come by and visit your Dad. I've been missing my 'too busy' son. I'd like to talk to you about the joy in using that authority you don't know you have—and the consequences."

#   #   #

Willie lay quietly, his breathing labored, staring up at the ceiling. Brad came in carrying a black back pack and hung it on the corner of the bed. "Hey, Willie, I brought your stuff. How's it going?"

"How's it look? Your prayer didn't work."

38

"Sorry. It looks like your liver's been in combat for awhile. Doctor Gordon is watching your response to his medicine."

"Yeah, well…" Willie turned away and spoke quietly to the wall. "Doc said I probably don't have long to live." He choked back a sob. "Course I don't have much to live for anyway."

"We'll see about that." Brad sat on the edge of the bed and leaned toward him with narrowed eyes. "Willie, if you were a billionaire, how much would you pay right now for the secret to living forever?"

"Huh?" Willie's lips tightened as he thought about it. "At least five hundred million. I'd give it all if I could sell the secret to others."

"Sounds logical--worldly thinking, but logical." Brad nodded. "Well, you're in luck. I'm going to sell it to you for the same price I paid."

Willie chuckled. "The only problem is I've got twelve fifty in cash and there's no such thing anyway."

"More good news. You get to keep your cash and you get a new body to replace the one you've been beating to a pulp. Besides that, you can share the secret with anyone you like."

"Ahh," Willie pointed at him. "You're still selling that Jesus thing, aren't you?"

"I am, and I'm willing to be patient and persistent, but it seems you're out of time, Willie."

"Okay, I'll listen, but why would God want to keep a guy like me around?"

"First, God loves you and has a special plan just for you. He wrote it down before you were born. Jesus knows you have *far* more potential than you ever dreamed. It's His desire that everyone should come into repentance and be saved."

"I guess.'

Brad's expression showed pain and compassion. He took hold of his shoulder. "Ah, Willie, all you have to do is accept Jesus as your Lord and savior and I'll lead you through the prayer. Ready?"

Now alert and attentive, Willie nodded.

"Hang on." Brad grinned. "A new person is about to be born."

NINE

Jackie thought she had arrived early in the garden, but Gina was already there, pacing along the back fence and talking to herself. The artist searched for a subject, found something that interested her in the bushes by the palm tree and set up her easel nearby.

Before the charcoal sketch was finished, Gina collapsed on the bench, head in her hands. Jackie worked on her background colors and thought she might get her attention by quietly singing "How Great Thou Art."

As the details began to appear on the canvas, Gina came over, stood behind her and peered at the developing work. "Now yer drawing *spider webs?*"

Jackie turned and knocked her back a step with an awesome smile. "I know they're just insects, but I'm fascinated by the perfection of their web design."

"They're not insects. They are arachnids."

"Well, there we go again…" Jackie giggled. "Learned something else. You love to teach, don't you?"

There was that flicker of a smile again. "But why did you draw water on it? I don't see any."

41

"Well, when I first came, the sprinkler had hit it and little drops were sparkling in the sunlight."

"Humph. Well, as long as you're at it, why not paint the spider that made it?"

"I would, but I don't see him."

"*Her,* you don't see her. The females make the webs."

"Wow." Jackie spread her arms, paintbrush held high. "You studied biology, huh?"

"Yeah." A real smile this time. "It was my major at USC."

"Now I'm impressed. Love to hear about it if you want."

Gina dismissed the subject with a hand gesture. "Never mind. Anyway, I think you should paint her in."

"From my imagination?"

"No." She pointed to the edge of the web. "Follow the support line. She's peeking out under that hibiscus leaf, just waiting for her next victim."

Jackie gave her a wide-eyed look, dropped down on one knee and looked up under the leaf. She came up with her mouth open in amazement. "I *saw* her. She's big and red. Wow, Gina, thanks. You make science fun. I'll bet if you were my teacher I'd have gotten better than a C+."

Gina turned her gaze toward the overhead clouds, a thin painful smile on her lips, but when she looked down, her expression had faded to gray. "It's about time to go in, but, I'm sure you didn't get a contract to illustrate a Biology text. Why take all that time to paint this?"

Jackie grinned. "Because I can see beauty in all of God's work. He gave little Miss spider a special talent. To me, her web is a beautiful marvel of inspired architecture. Gina, can you see anything in it beyond the science—a message, perhaps an emotion?"

"Oh, sure." Gina sighed and turned a dark, angry gaze toward the artist. "I see entrapment followed by *death*."

TEN

"Here, Carla, you can smudge off some excess charcoal before you add paint." Jackie dabbed at her student's Gessobord surface with a rag then handed it to her. "You try it."

"Do you think a flower vase is too dull for a subject?"

"Not at *all.*" She shook her head. "You're gonna make those flowers dance the rumba with castanets. Picture them in your head first."

Jackie leaned in behind another student to watch her making a pencil sketch. "A mother dog and puppies—that's pretty ambitious at your stage, but I love it, Sissy."

Sissy pulled out a magazine page from her pocket. "I liked this picture but I want more puppies looking out."

"Okay, wait a sec." Jackie went to a nearby drawer and returned with a clip. She clamped the photo to the top of the easel. "Start with a light touch. You can erase and play with it until it looks right. I'll bet you'll have a puppy jumping into my lap before you're done."

Sissy giggled. "But you'll have to help me when I paint the fur. I have no idea."

44

"That'll be the easy part. Start with the base color you want then give me a holler. Good work, Sissy."

Jackie moved behind an artist who was making sweeping strokes on a large canvas. "Mary, that's gonna be *gorgeous*. You've been painting awhile, haven't you?"

"Haven't had much chance lately, but yes." She made a few strokes on a mountain but suddenly froze and turned sad eyes toward her teacher. "I need this. It helps me forget."

"Jackie smiled, despite her look. "But while you're forgetting, you're bringing something new and beautiful into the world." She leaned in to take a closer look and let out a little squeak. "Oh, that's brilliant. Way down in that enormous canyon, you've drawn attention to a person in a little pink boat. I love it, but why is the boat sailing sideways?"

Wistful eyes turned her way. "Cause it is adrift, Jackie."

Martha Eldridge stood in the doorway and interrupted them. "Hi, ladies. I just want to remind you all of the street fair two weeks from Saturday. We'll drive any of you who want to go in our vans. You can sell your artwork at our booth, and there will be lots of food and live music. I hope all of you will come."

Happy paint brushes waved in the air. Martha smiled and pointed to Jackie. "Can you drop by my office after?"

#   #   #

Jackie bounced into Martha's office. "Hi, that street fair sounds like so much fun. Is it just for the homeless?"

"Oh, no. Everyone is invited but we promote it for them."
She came around her desk with Keepher to greet Jackie. "There's
going to be several churches involved and fun things for the kids too
like pony rides. I'm supposed to monitor their bouncy house."

Jackie bent down for a kissy-face moment with the dog.
"Ooh, I hope I'm not too big for those."

Martha laughed. "You *are*, silly, and I'm assigning you to
manage the grade school kids."

Jackie pouted then burbled her lips. "Aw, I gotta be grown
up, huh?"

"Don't fret. They'll love you." She pointed a finger. "Listen,
I want to thank you for taking time with Gina."

"Hmph." Her face fell. "She's in a real dark place, Martha. I
really don't know if I'm helping her at all."

"Not true. I've been peeking out the window and I think
you're doing great." Martha answered her puzzled look. "Gina has
been around for two years now. You are the first person she's even
given more than a grunt and one word answers to. You got her
talking. That's really something."

Jackie squinted at the ceiling in thought. "I did catch
something about her. The only times I've seen her smile is when she
realizes I'd looked up a word she'd used or when she teaches me
something. Gina has the heart of a teacher and she's smart, Martha,
but I think she must have been through some terrible things."

"One can only imagine. Did you see the scars on her wrists? Suicide attempts."

"Yuck." Jackie looked down and shook her head. "Well, if she comes by again, I'm planning a surprise for her."

Patricia, a woman on Martha's staff, stood in the doorway and waved at them. "I've got another surprise for you guys. The police are on the way. We got trouble brewing in the bunk room."

Martha's hand went to her cheek. "Oh, no. It's not Judy Price again, is it?"

The two rushed out leaving Jackie and her puzzled expression behind. When they approached the room, Judy was shouting. "Yeah, why didn't you just tell the whole f--- world! You b---!"

Judy sported a man's haircut, jeans and a rock band T shirt. She had a woman pinned against the wall, shouting at her, inches from her face. "You could-a just said no thanks, but *no*, you wanted to be some righteous *hero*, huh?"

The woman pleaded, "But I, I just asked Patricia to speak to you." Judy slammed the woman's shoulders against the wall. "Oof."

"Yeah, well there's a bunch of customers in here. You gonna rat on them too?"

Patricia and Martha sprinted toward them, Martha calling out, "Okay, Judy, just back off, okay?"

Judy gave the woman a last shove and turned to face them. She was unsteady on her feet and her eyes rolled around the room.

"Well, well, here comes administration. What ya gonna do? Pray at me or kick me out again?"

Martha spoke in a soft but firm tone. "Both, I think, Judy. You're clearly back on drugs, and now you're violent and selling them, too, aren't you?"

Judy stepped toward them. "You call *that* violent?" She grabbed an umbrella lying on a nearby cot and swung it around in menacing circles. "I'll show you violent."

Two female policewomen rushed in the door, one shouting, "Hold it right there, lady."

Judy glowered at Patricia and Martha. "Oh, great—the cops. You think you're helping people? You're not."

The police quickly handcuffed Judy. One recited the Miranda rights and the other spoke to Martha. "I'll be back in a moment to take some statements. We know this one and we're getting a warrant to search her belongings."

Martha said, "We had Judy in a rehab two months ago, but she didn't stay."

"Lotta that going on, M'am."

Judy began to twist and squirm as they walked her out. She cried out. "This is a *prison*, ladies. See what happens when you try to be free?" She turned her head back to the bunk room just before being dragged out the door. "I'll be back tomorrow with some more 'freedom'—just wait."

As the police women loaded Judy into the car, one tried to make eye contact. "What part of 'anything you say can and will be used against you' didn't you understand?"

ELEVEN

Brad's shift was over and now he sat beside Willie's bed, leaning toward him. The patient lay semi-conscious, his breathing labored. Suddenly Willie convulsed into awareness, coughed, and looked around.

His gaze fixed on Brad and he spoke in a loud whisper. "What are you doing here?"

"I've been praying for you."

"Yeah, well, looks like I'm dying anyway."

Brad raised a finger. "I'll rebuke that remark. My Dad says words are important. Let's use positive ones."

"Sure." He rolled his eyes. "I'm fresh out of 'positive.' You try."

Brad smiled and gave his arm a pat. "Last time we talked you repented, forgave those who hurt you and accepted Jesus as your Lord and Savior. The Kingdom is now your home, Willie. You've got eternal life."

"Well, I..." Willie began coughing and leaned up on one elbow. Brad handed him a tissue. "Don't get me wrong, Doc. I don't want to sound like a doubter. At least I'll sidestep Hell when I die, right?"

"Yeah, that's a big positive, isn't it? And along with immortality comes a whole new body, but I don't believe you're leaving this Earth as soon as your doctors think."

"Good." Willie tried a smile but it became a grimace. "A new body, huh? How about asking God for a new liver as a down payment?"

"Maybe." Brad chuckled and opened his hands. "I've been learning about a new, authoritative way to pray. Mind if I try it out on you?"

"Knock yourself out."

"Okay, but first it's important to believe. I believe in my heart that God desires to heal you, but do *you* believe it?"

"Ahem." A nurse stood in the doorway with a medicine cart. "Are you going to be done soon? It's time for his meds."

"Sure." Brad waved her in. "You can give them to him and join us in prayer therapy if you like."

"Aah…" The nurse shook her head and burbled her lips. "I'll be back in ten. Just finish up, okay?"

Brad turned back to Willie and smiled. "I think we were at the belief in healing question."

Willie slumped back and looked at the ceiling for a few moments. "He's my Savior, right?"

"Absolutely."

"And now that I've been forgiven, He loves me, right?"

"God loved you before too, but right."

"Okay, so I believe he wants me to be well, and I *know* He has the power."

"Right on." Brad gave him two thumbs up. "And He will work through believers such as ourselves for His purpose. The Bible says that for those who call upon His name, He will arise with healing on His wings."

Willie tilted his head. "Jesus' got wings?"

Brad chuckled. "I don't know, but that's what it says. Anyway, right now I want you to think healing."

"Thinking and believing, Boss."

Brad stood up, placed both hands over Willie's liver and declared in a loud voice: "By Willie's faith and the power vested in me, I declare this man *healed* in Jesus name."

A woman in a room across the hall cried out, "Halleluiah!"

Willie grinned. "Whoa, thank you, man. That tingled."

"My pleasure. Say, George has been keeping an eye on the rest of your stuff. Do you want it moved somewhere until you get back?"

"I like that 'until I get back' idea. Tell him to fold up my tent and keep in next to him. There's not much inside, but maybe you could put it in a plastic bag, huh?"

"Will do. Keep the faith, my friend. I'll check back with you tomorrow."

# # #

George was up and doing stretching exercises the next morning. He continued bending his well muscled black arms and legs when Brad talked to him. "Hi, George, getting ready for the marathon?"

"Sleeping on concrete will leave you stiff. What can I do for you?"

"It's for Willie. He'll be awhile. He wants me to put his stuff in a bag and hold it for him. Could you fold his tent and keep it near you?"

"Really?" George stopped. "Word on the street is he's already ashes."

"Don't believe rumors. Say, George, can I ask you a personal question?"

"Shoot."

"You seem different than the others here in the alley. What's your story?"

"Different?" He chuckled. You mean because I'm black, handsome and fit, or all of the above."

Brad chuckled. "Well I won't argue with that, but I think you don't use drugs and you seem well adjusted."

"Yeah, I got plans to move up, and I'm working two jobs."

"Two?"

"Yup, one is looking after this alley. You wouldn't believe how many come by to steal stuff. The other is cleanup at Chick-fil-A after they close. Most wouldn't hire a guy like me, but they did."

"So you have an income and plans. That's great. Do you believe in God?"

George laughed. "I knew that was coming. What took you so long? Yeah, I believe in God and Jesus is my Savior. I even wander into that church across the street once in awhile."

Brad nodded. "I sort of sensed that—course that angel sculpture I see peeking out of your tent was a clue."

George opened his tent with a grin and a dozen fired clay sculptures came into view. "Maybe this is job number three, but right now it's a hobby. Mister Cummings at Woodrow Junior High lets me use his kiln. He gives me the clay too."

Brad got down on his knees to admire the display. "I'm impressed, George. I love this angel. Your work is really professional."

"Two hundred bucks and she's yours."

Brad stood up and laughed. "A bit out of my league right now."

"For you, one hundred, and I'll put it on layaway until you can afford it."

"Okay," He pointed at him. "But it just occurred to me, there's a church fair on Saturday the fourteenth. I'll take you there if you want and you can sell your sculptures at our church booth. Not only that, I hear there's free food."

"Hey, you're on, brother."

TWELVE

The lawn garden beside the church welcomed visitors with the scent of Jasmine and a warm breeze, gently swaying the overhanging palm fronds. Jackie arrived on her teaching day with her arms full of supplies. One of her pupils saw her struggling with the latch and opened the gate for her. She was rewarded with a wide grin. "Thanks, Carla. Are you ready for your lesson later?"

Carla took the easel out of her arms. "Sure, 'Teach,' but I finished that lion head so I'll be looking at a blank canvas."

"I see." Jackie squinted at her. "Unfortunately, I don't allow for artist block. As I said last week, our next subject will be from your imagination, so get it crank'n. Just look past all the blank whiteness and wait for that fascinating picture to appear."

Carla scowled. "Uh, I don't know, Jackie."

"Ah, don't worry, I'll assign you something if you don't get an inspiration."

Carla placed Jackie's easel beside the corner bench and gave her a pained smile. "Actually, I've been thinking of some weird stuff. Hope you won't mind."

"Nope, just so long as it's PG-13."

"Okay." She chuckled and headed back to her friends near the gate.

Jackie sat back on the wrought iron seat and a few enjoyed lungfuls of fragrant air. There was no sign of Gina. *After that last tense moment we had, I wonder if she'll even show up.* She leaned toward her easel, her mind already envisioning an image. She began a pencil sketch--a half circle at the bottom and clouds at the top.

Gina lumbered in with her usual somber expression. "Hi, Gina." Jackie delivered her trademark, thunderous smile. "Good to see you."

Hands on hips. "Have you *ever* been sad, kid?"

"Oh, my gosh, Gina—big time. Most men I like treat me like I'm a boy. The last one liked soccer, but when I asked him to come and see me play, all I got back was 'too busy'."

"But you get over things like that, don't you?"

"Yeah, I remember the good things, my hopes for the future, and most of all, I remember that God loves me. His plan is always better than what we come up with on our own." She went back to her sketch.

"Uh, huh." Gina glanced at the canvas and slumped onto the edge of the bench. A face was beginning to emerge through the clouds "Whatcha working on? Is that gonna be a fortune teller?"

Jackie kept drawing. After a few moments she responded with a quiet, "Nope."

"A genie, maybe?"

A pause, a shake of the head, and a few more strokes: "Nuh--uh."

The face of a handsome, bearded man looking down began to appear, his arms curved downward. Gina ventured, "A king on his throne surveying his lands?"

"Ah, you're getting closer now. Sometimes I paint what God shows me in my head."

The arms were reaching down with open hands, and the circle became the earth. Gina scowled, sat back on the bench and dropped her head. Jackie added some details in silence. Finally, she put her pencil down and announced. "Today I see God reaching down and surrounding Earth with His love."

Gina sat motionless. Tears began to stream down her cheeks with hiccupping sobs. Jackie put her pencil down, slid over and placed a gentle hand on her shoulder. Through the course weave of her dress, she could feel the older woman quaking. "Oh. my gosh, Gina? What do *you* see?"

Gina turned a tormented face toward her and almost shouted, "Judgement!" Then in a croaking whisper, "Horrible judgement, and don't think you can save me with that love talk."

Jackie gently massaged her shoulder and spoke softly. "I can't, but I know *He* can. I know there's no sin stronger than God's Grace. Can you tell me about it?"

Anger burned in her face. Gina pulled away from her touch and glowered at Jackie. "I'm going to burn in *Hell*, Jackie. That's why I'm afraid to kill myself."

"Tell me."

"…No."

Jackie took her unwilling hands in hers and stared with resolute patience until she made eye contact. "Tell me," she whispered.

"…There's—there's lots of things—lots. Murder, for one."

Now wide-eyed, Jackie said, "Okay, you got me shocked, but what you say will *never* be repeated."

"I, I didn't pull any triggers myself. I was about twelve--living with my mom and stepdad. There was this guy in the neighborhood, a real creep, and we were all afraid of him."

Gina paused. She turned her head skyward, but her eyes were closed. Finally, she released a big breath. "One night I heard arguing outside my window and I saw the bad guy under the streetlight. He was holding a gun on some man. The man tried to bolt away but he shot him in the back—dead."

"That's horrible, but *you* did nothing wrong."

"Yeah, I did. I didn't say anything because I was scared of him."

"You were *twelve* and in a bad neighborhood. I might have done the same thing, but you could still report it now."

"The man died in a shootout with police the next year."

"Okay," Jackie sighed and released her hands with a pat. "So, case closed."

Gina shook her head vigorously. "I wish. No, one of the policemen was killed too. His name was Sean O'Rourke, age twenty six with a wife and a two year old boy."

Jackie dropped her head and took her hands back with a squeeze. "Oh, gosh." She bit her lip and her head shivered. "Now I understand. Sean would be alive, but you *must* forgive yourself. You've repented. Forgive your twelve year old self. God does."

Gina began sobbing loudly. Other women in the garden looked on but kept their distance. Jackie moved closer and embraced her until the crying subsided.

Gina shook her head. "B-but that's only the beginning." She inhaled through her nose with a snuff. "I didn't report my step father for molesting me, and I had an abortion in college. Now that *is* murder, right?"

Jackie nodded, deep concern on her face. "Anything else?"

"Okay, you ready for this? Step dad left and when my mother committed suicide my senior year, I started selling drugs and prostituting to pay for my expenses. "

"Yuck, but then you graduated, right? Did you get a job?"

"Teachers assistant at the college. Lasted ten minutes. I'd started using myself and I got busted for selling. That put me in jail for a few years. There--enough sins for you?"

Jackie sat up straight and exhaled loudly. She pulled out a tissue and wiped off a tear on Gina's cheek, then one from her own. They sat in silence for a few moments. Jackie spoke in a croaky voice. "I see two good things."

Gina crossed her eyes and returned a 'now I *know* you're crazy' look. "No, really. First, it's clear that you believe in God and fear Him. Second, you're obviously repentant. Also I think you're off the drugs, right?"

"I'm off, and, yeah I wish I'd made better choices, but I can't change the past. So your *good* news is that while I flutter down into the lake of fire I can holler 'Sooreee!' all the way down."

Jackie snorted and suppressed a grin. "Gina, hasn't anyone told you why Jesus died on the cross?"

"Maybe so He could say He suffered more than any of us punks, and we should quit complaining."

"Nope. He willingly gave His *life* for us punks out of love. Despite His sinless life, He took on *all* of our sins—all yours too-- and sacrificed Himself in complete atonement for those sins so that anyone who believed and followed Him would be forgiven and have *His* righteousness and eternal life."

"All *my* sins? Musta missed that course in college. Sounds too good to be true."

"But, it *is* true—all your sins and even far worse sins out there in the world. I know Jesus loves you just as you are, Gina, and He wants a personal relationship with you. In your next quiet moment, ask Him if He's really there. Ask Him to reveal Himself. Ask for forgiveness and the strength to forgive those who've hurt you. Can I pray with you?"

Gina looked into her eyes, her expression slowly changing to calm. Without speaking, she reached for Jackie's hand.

THIRTEEN

On his way past the nurse's station, Doctor Gordon waved him over. "Brad, I want to show you something before you go in and see your friend."

He punched up an image on the monitor. "This is William Clark's original abdominal film showing a shrunken liver, but note the white lines going through it. This likely indicates a digital transcription error so I ordered an MRI this morning. His liver is actually normal."

A sly grin spread across Brad's face. "And I assume you repeated the hepatic and pancreatic enzymes, too?"

"Yes, they're normal too, and here's a learning point for you. When you see readings that are so high and off scale, always repeat them. The machine that analyses the blood is automatic and any machine can malfunction."

"So," He raised his hands. "You're saying Willie is well now?"

"He wasn't really sick. I believe they mistook an alcoholic bender with illness in the ER, especially when they looked at the faulty enzyme results. He might be 'schizo', however. He's been dancing around his room praising God."

Brad couldn't suppress a laugh. "So, he's ready for discharge?"

"Absolutely, but Social Services can't find any relatives."

"Ask them if he can go home with me after my shift. I know where he hangs out."

"Should be fine. I'll be glad to see him go. He's been trying to evangelize me and everyone in sight."

When Brad stood at the entrance to Willie's room he found him standing on his bed pretending he was surfing. Brad raised his arms. "Hey, hey!"

Willie jumped off his bed and shook his hands in the air. "Halleluiah!" He embraced Brad. "You *healed* me, Doc."

"No, *God* healed you, but through both our faiths."

Willie let go of him and spun around. "I know, I know. Anyway, it's a miracle."

"Praise the Lord. Look, when I get off this evening, you're coming to my place for a couple of days. I want to get you some decent clothes and we can talk about where you go from here."

Willie suddenly stopped, confronted Brad with wide eyes and whispered, "Doc, I *met* Him last night."

"Met who?"

"Jesus. He was standing in front of me just like you are right now—only taller: light beige fluffy shirt—purple sash. He said either way I'd have a new life ahead of me, but I could either go with Him now or I could choose to start that life here on Earth."

"Wow, and you chose to stay on Earth."

"His gaze goes right through you, doc. It's like He can see your inner soul. When I stood in His presence—I, I can't say it in words—it just felt wonderful."

"I can only imagine. Did Jesus say anything else?"

Willie looked up at the ceiling and did a tap dance in place. "Before He left, He put His hand on my shoulder and said, 'Go in peace and tell them of my love.' Then I woke up in bed feeling great."

Brad's pager buzzed. He gave Willie a few pats on his shoulder. "Gotta go. Remember, God will never leave you, man. I'll be back in a couple of hours when you're discharged."

#   #   #

The pager was from his supervising physician, Doctor Jim Sewell, asking him to report to him ASAP and he found him at the nurse's station. "Hello, Jim. You know I'm off duty soon, but if there's an emerg…"

"No, no." He motioned for him toward a more private part of the station. "Look, Brad, this is just a heads up about the hospital director. Personally, it doesn't bother me, but he told me there have been complaints about your proselytizing patients."

"You mean because I prayed with some of them?" Brad stood erect. "Sir, I never forced myself on anyone and it never impacted my medical care."

65

"You don't have to convince me, son. You're a great PA, but I'm just telling you to be discreet about anything openly religious around here. Personally I appreciate it, but there are some who are easily offended."

"Okay." Brad sighed. "I'll be more careful, but if you want to look at an interesting prayer result, check out William Clark's file. He wasn't my patient, medically at least, but he was—well, judge for yourself."

"Will do. The Director will likely ask to see you. Just so you know, he has been known to over react."

FOURTEEN

On the next Art School night, Gina entered the garden and found Jackie standing up at her easel facing the gate. She strolled over and asked, "Whatcha working on tonight, Miss smiley-face?"

Jackie peered over the top of her drawing. "I'm doing one on prophesy. Come around and see."

Gina squinted at the work. "Oh, portraits—a happy woman and a sad one. Who are they?"

"It's not finished. Give me a little time and see if you recognize anyone." Jackie resumed sketching. "How are you feeling today?"

"Better, but kinda strange too." She took a step to one side and looked out at the street. "I've had moments when I've actually felt peaceful. That's good--haven't felt that way in a long, long time, but then I slip back into the gray world."

Jackie gave her a sideways glance. "Sounds to me like you're on the fence between two worlds. Did you try that Jesus prayer?"

"I thought I was being kinda silly asking if someone was there, but, yeah; I did. No answer."

"Keep trying. God is in a dimension we can't see, but once in awhile He gives us a peek. There are times He'll use words, but more often He'll talk to you with a feeling, or just an urge to do something. I think the important thing is that He wants a relationship. Personally, I've discovered He loves us all something awful, Gina."

"Humph." Gina put her hands on her hips, leaned in at the drawing and whispered, "Long ago I faced the reality that no one could love me."

Jackie made eye contact and pouted at her. "No, no—not true. Anger like that only pushes people away. Anyway, I like you."

Gina chuckled. "But we all know how weird *you* are." She pointed at one portrait. "Say, the woman on the left looks a lot like me—and so does the other one--except for the silly grin, of course. I don't have a sister."

"There, finished." Jackie bestowed another earthquake smile. "I told you, this drawing is prophetic. They're pictures of you before and after." She reached for her cell phone. "I have a song I'd like you to hear."

"Not one of those sappy love songs, I hope. I hate them."

"This one is by Lauren Daigle. It's supposed to be Jesus speaking."

She turned up the volume on Lauren's lovely, quavering voice as she sang, "Though you have been broken—your innocence stolen—I hear you whisper—I hear your SOS."

Gina's expression became pained as Lauren sang the chorus loudly: "I-- will--*send* out an army—to *find* you--in the middle of the darkest night. It's true. I will rescue you."

Tears began to stream down Gina's cheeks as the song continued. "You're not defenseless—I'll be your shelter—I'll be your armor. I'll never stop marching to reach you—in the middle of the hardest fight. It's true. I will rescue you."

Gina began to laugh, tears still streaming. She embraced Jackie. "Oh, God, oh I'm here, dear Jesus. *Yes*."

FIFTEEN

Brad and Willie walked into the alley on the Saturday morning of the fair looking for George. They found him down a ways comforting the crazy one who was ramming his head against the new Port-a-Potty.

Brad joined in, grasping his shoulders from behind, pulling him back and gently rocking him back and forth. "Hey, man, easy, man."

The man stopped and turned to them, wild desperation on his face and a stream of blood flowing off his forehead. George spoke in a low tone. "We got you now, Bert. You'll be okay."

"They're coming for us all. It's all coming down real soon."

Brad took a tissue from his pocket and applied it to his forehead. "Bert, you've got a nasty open gash, my friend. Who is your doctor?"

"Goldstein, but I'm not going back there. We better find a cave up in the hills."

"You don't like him, or is it just his pills?"

"The pills! I can't hear them talking when I take them, so how can I protect myself? They're coming soon." He searched the perimeter. "Better watch out!"

George started to say, "But what the pills do…"

Brad interrupted. "Say, Bert, lets all go for a walk and check things out. The three of us can look around better, and you'll be safe with us."

Bert began to sway back and forth. He looked all around and up and down. "Okay but I ain't leaving my stuff."

They walked with him to his tent. Bert removed a plastic grocery bag and clutched it to his chest. He looked from one to the other, suspicion showing on his face. "Where are we going, huh? Better not be Goldstein."

Brad removed the tissue still stuck on Bert's forehead and showed him the blood. "I'm a medic. We're just going where I can put a dressing on your cut."

Bert turned to George. "You're coming too, right? I don't know him."

"I won't leave you, Buddy."

"Okay."

A fresh trickle of blood appeared. Brad reapplied the tissue and left it there. They headed down the street toward the hospital but Brad let them get ahead so he could talk in private on his phone. "Maggie, is that you at the ER desk?—I'm bringing in a patient with a laceration so I'll need a small surgical tray."

"Thanks, Maggie. Names Bert—probably Bertram. He's a Psyc patient of Doctor Goldstein. I'm sure they'll know who he is. He's off all his prescriptions and he better have a tranquilizer shot.

71

Could you call him and get authorization for it?—Yes, of course, someone from their department should come and see him. He's become a danger to himself and they'll probably admit him, but I'd suggest they wait until he's mellow. I'd like to finish my sutures first."

Bert balked as they stood in front of the emergency room. He pointed at the building. "There's someone looking at us from that window—see?"

"Oh, yeah, man," George put a hand on his shoulder. "That's a nurse in this hospital. Don't worry. I know her. She's cool."

"It's okay then?"

"We'll be fine. Lets go in and let Brad fix up your noggin."

#   #   #

The ER nurse administered the tranquilizer phoned in from the Psychiatry Department and Brad McKinley, P.A. sewed up Bert's scalp laceration with the permission of the doctor in charge. Two orderlies helped the now docile patient into a wheelchair. He clutched his bag of possessions, waved goodbye to Brad—and everyone else he passed along the way.

Brad rejoined his companions in the ER waiting room. "We'll be a little late to the church fair but Bert's in good hands."

Willie asked, "I thought you had to have permission to get a Psychiatric admission?"

"Not if he's an immediate danger to self or others. Anyway, he didn't object. We can talk to him about finding a place to live when he gets out, but they'll have to stabilize him first."

George said, "Fine." He picked up a suitcase. "I don't want to walk any further. My sculptures are heavy. Where's your car?"

Brad grinned. "But, George, you build up your muscles every morning and it's only twenty blocks."

George grimaced. "Not funny. Seriously, where's your car?"

The three headed out through the ER's sliding doors. Brad said, "Wait here."

Willie shot the question. "Wait? Wait for what?"

"I called an Uber."

George chuckled. "You don't even own a car, do you?"

SIXTEEN

Jackie stood in the parking lot of Saving Grace Church beside the idling van. She waved at Gina who was gingerly making her way down the front steps. "Hurry up. Pastor Roger already left with the other van."

"Alright, already. These donated sneakers are squeezing my feet."

Jackie peeked in the back of the van, turned to look at Gina and grimaced. "Almost full of moms and kids back there. I'm afraid you'll have to ride shotgun with our evil headmistress."

Martha laughed from the driver's seat and patted the seat next to her as Gina climbed aboard. "Welcome, Miss Giannopoulos. I make no excuses for Jackie. You know her well."

"I do. I'm just glad she didn't introduce me as a knife-wielding suicidal maniac."

Martha guffawed and started down the driveway. She looked in her rear view mirror and called out, "Okay, everyone, fasten your seat belts."

By the time they reached the freeway ramp, Jackie had both the adults and children singing. Gina pointed her thumb toward the back and smiled. "Martha, just where *did* you find that one?"

"Oh, the Lord sent her to us. That's for sure. It seems we were taking our lives too seriously." She glanced at Gina with raised eyebrows. "And I'm pleased to see a, shall we say, a slight change in you recently. Did Jackie have something to do with that?"

"Yeah." Gina let out a breath, closed her eyes and thought about her transformation. "I was locked up into guilt but she showed me that Jesus covered all the sins of those who follow Him. I kinda new that from church, but I used to think it was a fairy tale.

"Last night I had a big repentant cry session, and I forgave some people who don't deserve it. Suddenly, I felt this peaceful presence inside of me, and--I heard a voice call my name."

Martha turned toward her for a moment. "Do you think it was Jesus?"

"Uh huh. He just said 'Gina,' and it's hard to describe— there was love all over my name when He said it, and for the first time in my life, I felt forgiven—completely forgiven."

"Oh, that's just *beautiful*." She shot her a sparkly-eyed smile. "You *must* tell Jackie. So, are you thinking about what you might do next?"

"I'm actually thinking about my future, and part of me can hardly believe I am."

Martha gave two thumbs up, momentarily releasing the steering wheel. "Halleluiah!" She quickly turned the van. "Oops, I almost missed our exit. So, tell me: what would you like to do in this new future of yours?"

"It might not be possible but I'd really like to complete my teacher's certificate and teach biology and earth science."

Martha's mouth gaped. "You've got a college degree?"

"Yes, in Bio Science and a minor in Education. But my resume is, you might say, kinda messed up."

Martha gave her a quick finger point and pulled the van into their destination. "Keep thinking positive, dear. As you know, you can get the certificate courses on line and you're welcome to use the computer in my office."

Son Rise Congregational was a large church with parking lots all around. A young man waved them toward one lot, already half full with fair goers and cars. He called out to them pointing toward the fair on the other side.

The adults unloaded boxes of wares they hoped to sell plus folding chairs and a table. One was assigned to walk Saveher on a leash. Jackie herded the kids together and guided them toward a large group of other children.

Gina walked beside Martha helping her carry the supplies. "I think these paintings should sell well, but balloon animals?"

"Oh, at five dollars each, they'll be gone in an hour. I wasn't going to let them sell one of them, but finally I said, why not?"

That earned a quizzical look. "Which one is that?"

"The one wearing boxer shorts. Remind me later. I'll tell you the story that goes with 'Mister Surprise'."

SEVENTEEN

From the front seat of the Uber, Brad briefed Willie and George who sat in the back with a suitcase full of sculptures. "Okay, guys, four churches who help the homeless are sponsoring this fair and it's been promoted widely. There'll be families and kids from all over and anyone selling stuff can keep all their profits. Of course everyone is encouraged to add to the donation boxes, and that cash goes to help the relief programs."

George gave a thumbs-up. "Me? I'm just hoping for a bunch of rich art collectors to show up."

"And I'll bet you'll be in luck."

George snapped the suitcase open and held up a sculpture wrapped in newspaper.. "Last chance to get your angel at a bargain price. What do you say?"

Brad laughed. "I'll give you a few hours to make a killing first." He pointed at them. "Pay attention. We'll go to my church booth first and you can help us get set up. The fair is over at five o'clock, so I want both of you meet me back at our booth a little before, okay?"

"George said, "Yeah, but what if I'm sold out and we get bored sooner?"

"Oh, really?" Brad wiggled his finger at him. "You'll find adult games and things to do, but you don't get your free lunch until twelve thirty and you're expected to attend the chapel service afterward."

Willie grinned. "And that's what I'm looking forward to."

George tilted his head at him. "Lunch or sermon?"

"Both, really." He chuckled. "Hard to believe, right?"

The driver dropped them off at the front door of Son Rise Church. As they headed toward the crowds, Brad pointed to a row of portable showers on one side of the parking lot. "That operation is run by a group called New Dignity. At their table you can pick out some donated clothing and they'll give you a free bag of toiletries."

Willie poked George. "Dibs on a warm jacket and a blanket."

"All yours, Buddy."

Brad pointed over the crowd. "Our church booth should be over there, lined up along the edge. Beyond the lot, there's a lawn where the kids can play."

Willie pointed. "Hey, look, there's a bouncy house. That looks like fun."

Brad chuckled. "Sorry. Kids only."

After greeting people he knew at his church booth, and setting up George's sculpture display, Brad and Willie were free to wander around on their own.

Out on the lawn area, Brad thought an older woman might need help. She was monitoring the children entering the bounce house and they all were trying to get in at once. She spoke with authority. "Uh, *uh*! Only two at a time, kids. I'll blow the whistle when time's up." He guessed she was doing just fine.

"Hello, my name's Brad McKinley. You're running a tight ship here but let me know if I can help with anything. My dad's the pastor at Christ Church. We operate a training center and job finding agency for the homeless."

"That's great, Brad. I'm Martha Eldridge." She shook his hand. "I'm in charge of operations at Saving Grace Church for homeless women."

While they talked, Brad couldn't help but notice a young blonde woman in the middle of the field. She was wearing white shorts, sporting a bouncy pigtail, and playing dodgeball with several kids. That was distracting.

Brad mumbled, "Uh, does your church work with the homeless too?"

"Oh, yes—didn't I just say…" She reached out for a young boy. "Hey! I better hold that cell phone when you're in there, mister. No telling where it might wind up."

She turned back to him. "Nice to meet you. Yes, Saving Grace operates a ministry for homeless women. We provide a dinner, overnight bunks, breakfast and, of course, spiritual support. We also have teaching classes."

"Wow, that's impressive--almost a complete home."

"Well..." She held a girl back who looked up at her with a pout. "You can't go in with a boy. Girls go in with girls only. Just wait 'til the next time."

Martha continued, speaking to Brad but his eyes were intently following the game led by the laughing, bouncy lady. "Well, we think of our program as transitional. It's no substitute for a real home." With his gaze fixed on the field, she wasn't sure he heard. "Uh, Brad?"

He turned back quickly. "Oh, sorry—so you give them a home."

"A temporary one. By the way, that's Jackie, our art teacher, you're watching."

"She certainly is a happy sort."

"Ah, she's one in a million. Check out our booth. We've got art work from her and her class on sale there."

Brad visited all the booths and bought some things as well. When he looked back at the field, the game was over, but he saw Jackie again. She was sitting in a chair away from all the activity. She had a dark haired girl in her lap who was crying. Jackie was consoling her, resting her cheek on the girl's head and speaking softly in Spanish.

Brad went into the sanctuary and spoke with the kitchen volunteers about locations where free breakfast was being served.

Some of them had been homeless themselves, even one who was now an assistant pastor.

When he came out, Martha motioned for him to come back over to the bounce house. "Could you spell me for just ten minutes? I need to find the person who's taking the shift before lunch break. She hasn't shown up."

"Sure. No problem."

Between his whistle blows he watched Jackie who was back on the field, playing another game with the kids. They were chasing one another and screeching with delight. At one point, two kids with balls chased her around the corner of the bounce house. She skidded sideways and lost her balance with a screech. Brad reached out to try and catch her as she fell, but he slipped in the attempt, and they both crashed to the ground, Jackie landing on top of him.

"Oh, my gosh, I'm so sorry," she said, touching his cheek. "Are you hurt?"

Brad got up, lifting her up in his arms. "I might have scraped my leg but that's all. You okay?"

It would have been appropriate for him to put her down, but he continued to hold her as they talked. "My name's Jackie—uh, thanks for saving me. I guess I was being careless. I owe you one."

The kids stood around watching them with scowls on their faces. One boy stuck out his tongue at them. Brad grinned as he slowly lowered her to the ground. "I'm Brad. I'll consider us even if I can take you out to dinner tonight."

She giggled. "Gonna make me suffer for it, huh?" Glancing past the cluster of children, she spied a friend and called out. "Carla, could you take these kids for a few minutes. Have them do coloring book time at the table by the church door."

Carla hurried over and stood in front of the kids. "Okay, guys, come with me. I know something fun we can do, and I promise you'll get Jackie back later." She herded them away but one little girl turned and gave Jackie a smile and a wave."

Brad grinned at Jackie. "I've been watching you. You sure are good with kids."

She shrugged. "My problem is I forget I'm not one of them. I..."

She pointed at his leg. "Oh, no, you're *bleeding*."

He looked down at a spot of blood by the cuff of his trousers. "Ah, it's just a scratch. No big deal."

"Nonsense. Come over to our booth. We have a first aid kit and Martha had all us volunteers take a course in how to use it."

"But..."

"No buts." She tied the opening of the bounce house closed, took his hand, and guided her willing patient to a chair beside her church booth. After retrieving the kit, she sat down cross legged in front of him. "I'll have this dressed up in just a minute."

Brad suppressed a grin—didn't want to show how much he was enjoying this. Jackie took his shoe off, placed his foot in her lap and slid up his pants leg. "Oh, goodness, this more than a scratch." She made a tsk, tsk sound and looked around for any more injury.

He peered down at his leg. "Well, maybe a little cut in the abrasion."

Jackie held up an alcohol pad for him to see. "This may sting a bit, but first I have to clean the area."

He intentionally let out a pitiful moan.

Jackie gasped. "Oh, sorry, sorry," and began to massage his calf.

Brad bit his lip to keep from smiling. "Yes, yes, that feels *much* better now."

Jackie put on some antibiotic ointment and held up a large gauze pad. "This is called an island dressing. It will keep your wound clean while it heals."

Finally, she wrapped his leg with a stretchy elastic bandage. "And this is called Kerlex. It's designed to keep your dressing in place. Leave this on for two days." She handed him some fresh dressings in a plastic bag. "There." She gave his foot a little squeeze-squeeze and put it into his shoe. "Do you need instructions on how to change it?"

"No, I'll be good."

"But, I'm sure many people don't know how to do it right. Maybe there's a nurse where you work. What is it you do, Brad?"

He allowed himself the grin. "I'm a Physician's Assistant."

Jackie burst out with a laugh and treated him to her wondrous smile. She gave his knee a little slap and got up. "Why, you *stinker*. You could have told me. I should be asking *you.* How'd I do?"

"A perfect job, and I learned something from your treatment besides. A little massage makes the pain go away."

"Oh, good." She grabbed his hand and pulled him away. "Before we go to lunch, I have to check on my kids. Want to join me?"

"Maybe, but…" He looked over at the bounce house and saw that some woman had opened it up and was tending the line of kids. "Okay, lead the way."

They approached a folding table with children quietly coloring. "Thanks for covering for me, Carla."

"No problem, Jackie. I'll watch them until lunch time." She put a finger to the side of her pursed lips. "But, aren't you going to introduce me to your new friend?"

Jackie shrugged. "What friend?" Carla's eyes rolled. "All right, Carla." She put a hand on Brad's shoulder. "This is Bradley. He's a Physician's Assistant."

Reaching out for a handshake, "Bradford, actually. Call me Brad."

"Hi, I'm Carla. Thanks for saving our art teacher."

"Should I have?" They laughed.

Jackie began to walk around behind the children, Brad following in her wake. "A red face, huh." She pointed at a drawing. "Is he embarrassed or maybe sunburned?"

The boy looked up. "He's an *Indian*. See, the other guy is a cowboy."

"Got it."

She moved to a girl whose face was inches from the paper. "Oh, I like those flowers on her dress. You added them all on your own, huh?"

"Yeah, I'd like a dress like hers, but Mommy can't afford it—or a house neither."

As the girl resumed coloring, Brad asked, "You should be wearing glasses, Sweetie."

"Uh, maybe, but I ain't got none."

Brad turned toward Carla. "Before you break for lunch, could you find out her full name and church sponsor for me. This girl is *so* getting glasses."

As they moved around the table, Jackie whispered in his ear. "Thanks, Brad. She's gonna get a new dress too—one with flowers on it."

An older boy in a well pressed Hawaiian shirt was busy coloring on a plain sheet of paper. "Ah ha," Jackie said. "What's your name?"

He looked up and smiled. "I'm Ronald. My dad's the youth pastor here."

"Well, I'm impressed. I see you did your own drawing before adding color, and it's very good."

Brad tapped the drawing with his finger. "Is that Snoopy in the airplane?"

"Well, yeah, Dude."

Brad chuckled. "So glad he's moved on from the doghouse." A bell rang out. He looked around. "What's that?"

Jackie's hands went up. "Oh, right. That's my cue. I have twenty minutes to eat before I have to start waiter duty." She grabbed Brad's hand. "Come on. Want to come?"

"Oh, sure. I'd love to help out."

"Good, and over lunch you can tell me more about this guy who goes about saving women."

EIGHTEEN

It was time for their evening date. Brad's driver had no trouble finding Saving Grace Church. The front door area swarmed with homeless women pouring in for their six o'clock dinner. He felt like an intruder as he walked into their activity building surrounded by all those women. They were chatting loudly and, of course, checking him out but, just inside, there was Jackie waiting for him with her big smile.

She opened apologetic hands. "Sorry you had to meet me here instead of my folk's house, but I had to finish some business."

He offered her an escorting elbow which she took and they went out amid a hushed chorus of giggles and oohs. *Don't these ladies have something better to do,* he thought. *Next comes the spotlight and the confetti.*

As they strolled along to the car waiting in the street, Brad said, "I made a reservation, but if you have somewhere in mind, we can go anywhere you want."

She stopped him with a pout and a sigh. "Well, since I'm supposed to be paying you back, you choose—this time." She winked.

"But, did you have some place in mind?"

"Well, since you asked, I happen to have Zagat's Guide to Five Star Restaurants in my purse."

He laughed. "Oops, never mind. You'll just have to pay me back at Luigi's."

Brad opened the back door to the Uber. "Your limo awaits, mademoiselle."

"Merci." Jackie giggled. "So, you're one of those city folks who doesn't own a car, huh."

Brad didn't respond until they were on the way. "Or, maybe I just wanted to be alone in the back seat with you."

She raised a finger and said, "Driver, stop the car," but it was a whisper.

#   #   #

They continued their growing relationship in a quiet booth at Luigi's over Chianti and a shared stuffed artichoke appetizer.

Jackie pulled off a leaf and nodded enthusiastically. "This is delicious. Now tell me more about that man God healed. Was he the one helping you take down your booth?"

"He was. I didn't have much time for the details over lunch. The man is Willie Clark and he was living in an alley near the hospital when I met him. He was trained in computer technology but alcoholism and drugs pretty much destroyed his liver, not to mention his life."

"And you can't live without a liver. I know that much."

"Right, so one day he collapsed. When I talked to him in the hospital, he knew he was dying."

"So you prayed for him."

"Yes, but my 'Dear God, heal him' prayer had no effect."

Brad enjoyed looking into Jackie's large questioning eyes. She said, "But he recovered later?"

"No, no change at all, so I asked for a little coaching from my dad who is a pastor. He advised bringing Willie to Christ first and then praying in authority."

"Authority? What's that mean?"

"Dad explained that the apostles weren't sent out to ask *God* to heal people. Jesus gave them, and all His followers, a delegated authority to heal. He told them to *go* and heal the sick in His name."

"So you prayed like that?"

"Prayed, believed and declared like that. Willie believed, too."

"Wow, so that's when Willie started to get better?"

Brad chuckled. "More than better. His liver became completely normal and Willie said he saw Jesus as well."

"Oh, praise the Lord." Jackie bounced in her chair and glittering eyes danced over her giant smile. "That's so *wonderful*."

As she was saying this, the waiter set down the main course in front of her, and gave Jackie a quick look. "It not only looks wonderful, Ms., but wait till you taste it."

Jackie and Brad laughed and thanked the waiter without explaining. She said grace and asked, "What is Willie doing now?"

"He's living with me for awhile and looking for a job in computer repair. I got him some good clothes for an interview. The guy is so enthusiastic he's downright bubbly."

"You know, Brad," Jackie swallowed a bite of shrimp linguine. "When you actually see God at work it uplifts your own spirit as well. Martha once assigned me to help a depressed woman who was obsessed with guilt. After she found the Lord and accepted the fact of being forgiven, she became a new woman right before my eyes. Before that, I felt so awkward in her company, but now I love chatting with her. She's smart, too—gonna be a teacher, I think." She patted her chest. "I get excited again just thinking about it."

"That's so cool. Say, I saw some of your student's art work at the fair, and I even bought one of their funky balloon creations. It's in the plastic bag next to me."

"Do tell," Jackie put her fork down and put a knuckle in her teeth. "And just which one did you pick out?"

"The gorilla. He's got a neat pair of Big Dog swim trunks, and they only wanted five dollars for him."

Jackie cringed at the thought of him looking under the trunks. She rested her face on one hand and gave him a wide-eyed innocent look. "Those balloons will loose their air in a few months—best if you keep him in a dark place away from heat and wind."

"Sure." He wondered why she looked anxious. "I saw you making these for the kids today. Did those balloon animals come from your art class?"

"Yup."

The waiter handed them dessert menus. Jackie, anxious to change the subject, said, "How about we split a crème brulee?"

The two spent some time talking and laughing about many things, but Brad thought she was getting tired when she began to respond with "Uh huhs" and twiddled her fork in an unfinished dessert.

Brad called Uber. The change in Jackie's demeanor grew darker on the car ride back to Saving Grace Church. She stopped talking completely, turned away and stared out the car window.

As they pulled into the parking lot, Jackie's blue Nissan was the only one there. In a strained monotone, she said, "Thanks for the dinner."

"Oh, you're so welcome. Look, I hope we can get together again soon, but I'm not sure where to reach…"

She stepped out of the car and her gaze seemed to be on the roof of the car when she said, "I'm heading back to college tomorrow."

"Okay, if you give me your number, I could call."

"I'm sure we'll run into each other again one day." She quickly slipped into her car, closed the door and started the engine.

Brad sat open mouthed and speechless. He could feel his throat tightening. "Where to, sir?" the driver asked.

My God, what did I do wrong? He thought. "Bennie's Bar, Fourth and Lincoln."

NINETEEN

Determined to break his reputation for being late, Brad was early on his way to work. George was doing pushups in the alley. "Hey, George, what's up?"

"Twenty eight, twenty nine—uff, thirty." He rolled over and sat against the building wall with a grin. "I sold all of my sculptures on Saturday."

"That's so great." Brad squatted down in front of him. "But on the way home you said you had one left."

"I do—the little girl praying, but if I can get it to Mrs. Eldridge, she said she'd have the cash to pay me this week."

"Hey." Brad opened his hands. "I know her. I'll drop it off for you."

"Thanks." He reached behind him and handed over the sculpture. "How did your date go?"

"Don't want to talk about it."

"Yeah, you do. Bad dates are the ones you should get off your chest. Besides, you know all about me. It's only fair." He flashed a wide, white grin.

Brad realized that talking might ease his pain. He let out a breath. "Well, at first we were having a great time. But suddenly she

93

got cold and walked away without even giving me her phone number."

"Too bad. I thought she was into you--a real peppy girl—average face but the rest of her, well—let's say, real nice."

Brad chuckled. "So, you were ogling my date, huh?"

"Course I was. Men are born with eyes, right? Do you think she's pretty?"

"George, when Jackie smiles at you, she's the most beautiful woman in the world." Brad shook his head like there was water in his ear. "Look, enough of this. I've got to go to work. I'll check in on Bert and give you a report."

"Before you go…" George ducked into his tent and came out with a ukulele. "Let me sing you a song to cheer you up."

"That's okay. I'll get over her in a year or two."

George gave a sympathetic nod and strummed a few notes. "My dad used to sing this one." He grinned and sang.

"It was just one of those things—just one of those crazy flings.

"It was great fun, but it was just one of those bells that now and then rings.

"It was just one of those things.

"A trip to the moon on gossamer wings.

"It was just one of those things."

George bowed and some men nearby clapped.

Brad returned a thin smile. "I get it: be glad about the good time and move on. Who wrote that?"

"A musical poet—Cole Porter."

#   #   #

After donning his uniform, Brad headed up to the Psyc Ward and found his patient finishing breakfast. "Hi, Bert, how's it going?

The man looked up, startled. He slid his chair away from the table. "Who are you?"

"It's all right. I'm Brad, a friend of George. He and I brought you in here."

Bert returned a vacant, puzzled stare. "Don't know you."

"That's okay." He smiled. "You were a bit dazed when you came in. I sewed up your scalp."

"Oh, I kinda remember that."

"Mind if I take a peek at your dressing?"

"Don't hurt me, huh?"

"I promise." Brad leaned toward him, lifted the corner of his scalp dressing and looked at his sutures. "Looking good, Bert. The nurse should take these out soon. How are you feeling?"

"Kinda swimmy headed, Doc." He looked around and shrugged. "But, fine, I guess."

Brad felt pleased at his great progress. "Yeah, you look a lot better. I heard your brother came by to visit you."

"Uh huh. It's been years since I saw him—used to live in his guest house."

95

"Really? Why did you leave?"

"Said I was acting crazy—kicked me out—well I think his wife did. I could hear her screaming at him about me in the main house."

Brad opened his hands. "But now you're better. Maybe you could go back."

"Mike said I could, but I'd have to get checkups and stay on my medicine."

"That's great." He shook two thumbs in the air. "I've been praying for God to help you out someway."

"Yeah?" Brad was startled to see Bert smile. "You think prayers make things happen?"

"Absolutely—because God answers prayers. Is it okay if I pray for you?"

Bert looked around furtively. "Wait. Right here? Is that allowed?"

"Of course." Brad wasn't real sure about the "of course." The ward nurse stood nearby with a scowl.

But Bert said, "Okay. Could you pray I never have to go back to the alley?"

Brad extended open palms toward him. "Dear Lord…"

# # #

"How are things going, Buddy?" Don greeted him when he walked into the locker room,.

"Good and bad, Don. Looks like one schizophrenic will be off the streets with a new chance for a life. Bad news is I thought I hit it off with a really great woman, but she dumped me on our first date."

Don's face squinched. "I hope you didn't drop one of your usual dumb comments, did you?"

"No, not this time—really. I felt relaxed around her. It was like we'd known each other a long time, but suddenly, at the end of our date, it went poof. She just said she'd be leaving--didn't even turn back to wave."

"First dates are always awkward. Some are afraid of jumping right into commitment. Give her some time then send her a friendship card--you know--the ones with a happy dog on it saying how glad you were to meet her."

"Wish I could. She left before I could even ask for her address or phone number."

"Shoot. Do you know where she works?"

"All I know is she's a senior at some college and wants to teach art."

"Ah, Brad," He shook his head. "Sounds like you're out of luck, pal."

"Yeah, I guess. I'll just get back to work and try to forget about her."

Brad changed into his surgical scrubs and met his physician mentor, Doctor James Sewell, in the OR scrub room. "What kind of case are we operating on today, Doctor Jim?"

The surgeon looked at Brad with deep concern. "I'll have to work without you on my first case, Brad. The hospital director just called and said he needs to see you—something urgent, he said."

"Doctor Khomeini? About what?" Brad thought, *I know I didn't do anything wrong and I've been on time lately, but this doesn't sound good.*

"He didn't say."

#   #   #

Brad stood in front of the Director's secretary, waiting for her to complete a phone conversation. He wasn't aware that she had noticed him but when she hung up the phone she promptly punched the intercom. "McKinley's here, sir."

After a muffled, coarse response, she pointed to the door without looking up. Brad said, "Thank you ma'am. God bless you."

She shook her head and turned her attention to the computer on her desk.

Director Hassan Khomeini greeted Brad with a hard stare. He had a full black beard and an olive complexion. Despite a thick cushion on his chair his shoulders barely rose above his desk. "McKinley, you *do* understand that this is a public institution receiving most of our operating expenses from the city and the state, do you not?"

98

"Yes, sir."

"Uh, huh." He nodded. "And you are aware of the constitutional principal of separation of church and state, are you not?"

"Actually, sir, those words are not in the Constitution. They were from a letter written by Thomas Jefferson a bit later to assure the clergy that the state couldn't persecute them for their beliefs."

"What?" Hassan crumpled a piece of paper and hurled it at the wastebasket. He missed. "Are you telling me you don't understand the First Amendment?"

"Sure I do. It says that Congress, and by inference State governments, can't establish one denomination over another, and they can't tell people of faith how to exercise their worship or restrict their freedom of speech."

Hassan swore at Brad. "McKinley, what makes you think you know more than the courts and the professors?"

Brad searched the Director's eyes with calm resolution. He wondered why they were having this argument. "Sir, you brought me here to discuss constitutional law?"

"Hassan's eyes narrowed and they had a staring contest. "The Hospital Board has been fielding numerous complaints about you. It's not your medical care. That's fine, but people have had to watch you praying for patients—praying *loudly*, I might add."

Brad grinned. "And prayer has helped them in ways beyond my expect…."

Hassan's fist hit the desk. "I'm not interested in your Christian claptrap. Look, mister, I'm doing what I can to keep you here. The Board is willing to accept a compromise. You can pray for whoever you wish, but *silently*. Neither the patients nor anyone nearby should have any idea about what you're doing in secret."

Hassan was puzzled as Brad looked at him, not in anger, but with compassion. There being no response from him, he added, "So, that's it. We'll allow you to stay on staff and no one will be offended. You'll agree to that, won't you?"

The words "religion--free exercise thereof" did a silent dance in Brad's head. "I'm afraid I cannot agree to that, sir."

A wan smile crept across the Director's face. "I expected you'd say that." He handed Brad a paper he had already signed. "You are terminated from hospital sponsorship. You will remove yourself and all your possessions immediately."

Brad was surprised by the calmness he felt inside. Why was this shocker was not causing him distress? "Yes, sir," he said.

TWENTY

Martha Eldridge was absorbed studying papers on her desk. Nearby, Gina sat at a table pecking away at a computer. Jackie was noisily banging through objects on a wall shelf, occasionally exclaiming "oh." or "Doggone it!"

Martha looked over her glasses. "Something I can help you with, dear?"

"Yeah, I gotta leave for college in an hour and I can't find my oil paints."

"Oh, I'm sorry. I thought you were leaving those for our next teacher. I asked the custodian to put them on the closet shelf in the art room."

"Well, shoot." Jackie slammed something down on the shelf. "Maybe you could' a told me, huh?" She brusquely left the room.

Gina said, "Something's wrong, Martha. That is *so* un-Jackie like. I'm gonna go talk to her."

She found Jackie in the art room standing on a stool and tossing things off a shelf into a cardboard box. Gina watched Jackie's anguished face for a few moments before she spoke. "Hey! I can tell my little savior is in trouble. Can you stop for a second and tell me about it?"

"It's nothing." Jackie jumped off the stool and closed up the box. "I'll get over it."

Gina went to her, put a gentle arm around her shoulder and walked her over to a bench to sit down. "Maybe all I can do is listen, but I'm not letting you disappear without your telling me what's bugging you."

Jackie looked at her, desperation on her face, a smear of tear driven mascara on her cheek. When hiccups and sobs began, Gina drew her close and let her cry. Finally, Jackie said in a croaking voice. "I'm a stupid *fool*, Gina."

"Well then, you've been fooling all of us around here." She squinted into her eyes, wiped her cheek with a tissue and thought for a moment. "Gotta be about a man, right?"

"The nicest man, like *ever*." Her head fell on her chest.

Gina smiled and nodded. "Thought so. At least that's an area of my expertise." She chuckled. "He didn't seem interested in you, or what?"

"No, no, he really seemed to like me and we had a date last night. Now I *know* I'm not pretty enough to hold onto a man like that, so I guess I gave him the brush off so I wouldn't get hurt."

"Well, that worked just fine, didn't it? Think of all the pain you saved yourself from." Gina sat upright and let out a breath. "I'm getting the picture. Lets take this one thing at a time. Do you know who Barbara Streisand is?"

"Sure. Mother has her Christmas album—plays it for a month every year."

"Do you think Streisand's ugly?"

"She's not glamorous, but she's got a cute face."

"Exactly, and she sure did pretty well for herself, hasn't she? You look a lot like her."

Furrows appeared on Jackie's brow. "Really? You think so?"

"I know so. Your problem is you aren't believing in yourself, and you're the one who taught me that with faith in God, all things are possible." She opened her hands. "Think about this. Are the beautiful women the *only* ones with loving relationships?"

"No, you're right. I know you're right. I've been a stupid jerk."

"You're also the one who told me how much Jesus loves us just the way we are. So, put on a Jackie smile, call him up and apologize."

"Good idea, but…" She shrugged. "I don't have his number or email either."

Gina thought for a minute. She smiled. "Got it. Do you think you could sketch a portrait of him?"

Finally, a "Jackie grin." "Oh, easy, peasy. I have his face memorized."

"And what are you going to do with that sketch?"

Realization came over her face. "Of course! I'll send him his portrait with my apology and he'll know I care. Brilliant, Gina. Thanks."

Gina gave her a quick hug. "There. That's that happy face we all love."

Jackie pursed her lips. "Ooh, one problem, though. I don't know where he lives."

"How about work?"

"You're brilliant again. He works at Los Angeles General Hospital. I'll send it there."

TWENTY ONE

Brad was stomping around in his apartment feeling sorry for himself on his day off when his cell rang. *"Hey, Doc, it's George. Can you get over here this morning? Got a sick cookie on my hands. Hoping you can help."*

"What's the story? Somebody I know?"

"I don't think you've met Jeff. He's a young guy—got no folks. He moves around a lot but stays in our alley some. Didn't pay no mind when he disappeared a few days back, but last night he showed up, lying on the sidewalk and out of his mind."

"Drug overdose?"

"Doubt it. He only used weed and seemed healthy as a horse. Now he's shakin' all over."

"Be right there."

George and another homeless man named Matt had Jeff wrapped up in blankets against the side of the building. Only curly, blond hair and desperate blue eyes peered out of the covers. He was shivering and moaning.

Brad squatted down beside him. "Hello Jeff. I'm a Physician's Assistant." He put his hand on the patient's forehead. "You've got quite a fever going on there. What have you been doing the past few days?"

"Don't know, Doc," he croaked. "Last I remember was d-days ago."

"Any coughing—shortness of breath?"

"Uh uh."

"Bowel movements?"

"Who knows?"

Brad sighed, studied his patient and thought for a moment. "Jeff, what's the last thing you remember before the blank out?"

"I remember talking with three cool guys. They were going to a concert with a rich friend--said I could come and get all the smokes I wanted."

"So you went along, huh?"

"Yeah. This stretch limo pulls up and we all got 'happy shots' along the way—uh, that's what they called 'em."

"Whiskey shots?"

"No, needle shots. That's the last I remember until I woke up on the street."

"And that's what—three days later?"

Brad looked at George who nodded. "Had to be at least three."

Jeff was having a shudder attack and Brad tightened his blankets. He squinted at Jeff. "Do you hurt anywhere?"

He replied between shudders. "Yeah—musta fallen---on my back---hurts when I move."

Brad began to unwrap a section of cover from his back. "Sorry, Jeff, gotta take a look at this."

A neat, white oblong dressing came into view, surrounded by a halo of hot red skin. "My God, guys. They took his kidney, and the site's infected."

TWENTY TWO

Jackie sat on her dorm room bed at Barden Christian College unpacking her things. Mom had slipped a jar of blackberry jam into her backpack, a sure sign she knew her daughter was upset.

Jackie tightened her lips. *You never miss anything, do you, Mom? Maybe I should have told you.*

Her roommate, Gabriele, bustled in dragging bags and luggage. "Hi, Jackie. How was your summer—mine was just *fab*—found this boy—well he found me--you know. We got an ouchy sunburn together—and OMG—he said he's picking me up for Thanksgiving—I said, how about Halloween—ha, ha—and—say…" She looked at Jackie and frowned. "You look grumpy. What's up?"

Jackie got up with a sigh. "Nothing much, Gabby. Can I help you unpack?"

"Nothing much?" Gabby spun a 360 on one foot and gave her a pout. "I know 'nothing much' when I see it. This is *much*. Just tell me, did a dog or relative die? Yes or no."

"No."

"Okay, good." She plunked a suitcase and a wardrobe carrier onto her cot and zipped them open. "If you really want to help you could hang up these skirts and dresses. I'll take the top two drawers again if it's okay."

"Oh, sure."

Gabby began to hum as she arranged the dresser drawers. "This is me being discrete, girlfriend. Notice how I'm letting you just *volunteer* to tell me about your calamity."

"Don't worry, Gabby. It's just a silly thing and I'm working it out. Looks like your blue skirt should be ironed."

Gabby closed the drawers, draped one arm over the dresser and faced her roommate. "Jackie, you know I'm a happy person, but next to you I come off looking like Eyoure. I've always told you about my problems, so now it's your turn. Don't make me get out my mind can opener on you."

Jackie chuckled. "So, no secrets, huh?"

"No secrets allowed—and I just saw a little smile peek through—besides I already know there's a man involved."

"All right, I give up." Jackie opened her hands. "So I botched up a first date, but I've got a plan to straighten it out."

Gabby came over, put an arm around her shoulders and said, "There, that wasn't so hard." She smiled at her. "Right away, there's good news, Jackie. First you actually *had* a date, in what—maybe a year? Second, you obviously like this guy. So, hit me with a name and a description."

"Oh yeah?" Jackie flashed a grin. "You first. Tell me about your 'Mister Thanksgiving'."

Gabby laughed. "Ah, Jackie lives again. Well, his name is Stan and he's all big muscles on the outside but soft and sweet on the inside. He owns a big sloppy bloodhound and loves him to pieces. His older sister has a six month old and you should have seen Stan carrying his baby niece all around and making funny faces."

"He sounds perfect, Gab. Well my guy's name is Brad..." She looked up at the ceiling and bit her lip.

Gabby, came back to her and restored her arm around her shoulders. "Oh, oh. That's a sexy name, Hon."

"Brad is sweet, and funny. He loves the Lord and we both work to help the homeless. I know he likes me and I *really* don't know why I blew him off at the end."

Gabby let her go and gave her a stern look. "No, we both *know* why. You're afraid of relationships that crash, so you cut them off the second you feel you're getting involved. Now tell me about your plan to get him back."

"Okay," She shrugged. "I confided in Gina, an older woman I grew to like this summer. She suggested I sketch his picture and send it to him with a nice note."

Gabby gave her two thumbs up. "Perfect. Now, I'm the writer so I'll help you with the heart-melting note. You get your sketchy pencil thing going, girl."

TWENTY THREE

"Look, he can't get up." George shook his head. "Should you call an ambulance?"

"No need. The hospital's just two blocks away." Brad stood over the man. "I'll be right back with a wheelchair."

"Word is they hate you now. You can get a chair?"

Brad thought, *I hope not everybody.* "We'll see."

He jogged over to the Emergency Room and approached Sally, a receptionist he knew. "Hi, Sally. I know I'm not on staff anymore but there's a man down the street with a high fever. He was attacked by kidney thieves and can't walk. Can I borrow a wheelchair to bring him in?"

Sally scooted around the counter and leaned in close to whisper. "I think it's a *terrible* thing that they let you go." She searched the room to make sure the nurse wasn't looking. "Here, Brad, take this gurney. I'll alert the surgeon on call."

George, Brad and Matt hoisted Jeff onto the gurney. He was now limp and semi-conscious, but as they wheeled him into the ER they were met by a nurse and Doctor Sewell. Antibiotics flowed into the IV as soon as it was hooked up and they rolled Jeff on his side exposing his bandaged back.

Brad explained to Doctor Sewell, "His name's Jeff. He was basically kidnapped and promised a weed party four to six days ago. Last night they dumped him back on the street."

They wheeled their patient behind the curtains of an ER stall. Sewell removed the dressing revealing a red incision with pus oozing out one end. "This is criminal, folks. Nurse, notify the police and request an ICU bed. Brad, get a culture on that drainage."

The doctor made eye contact with Brad when the nurse left. "Shall we pray for him, Brad?"

"Of course." They placed their hands, one on the patients head and one over his incision. Brad began: "Dear Lord, we cry out to you to have mercy on Jeff, the victim of a terrible crime. We thank you for the authority you have given your servants and we declare this man will completely recover in Jesus name."

Sewell said, "Well done, Brad. Can I talk with you in the waiting room after?"

"Sure. Doctor, what do you think his chances are?"

"We'll know more in twelve hours when we see his response to the antibiotics." He smiled. "The Lord will take care of the..."

The nurse poked her head through the curtains. "The police are here, and ICU is ready."

"Good, but the patient can't talk at the moment. Show them the wound before you send him upstairs. Brad will give them the story while I write his orders."

Brad wished he could go with the patient, but that would be reserved for the hospital staff. He waited patiently for his former mentor to return. What was he going to say?

When Sewell came back he motioned for Brad to follow him outside and greeted him with a smile. "Bradford McKinley, my favorite faith healer: good to see you again."

"Glad to feel useful again, sir."

"Remember, Brad, Jesus said if they persecuted me, they will persecute you also. Some in the administration are afraid of the healing they saw happen to William Clark. Have you been accepted anywhere else to complete your internship?"

"No, one refusal. I'm still waiting to hear from two others."

"Did you know that the Mainline Surgical Group I'm with is accredited to train Physician Assistants?"

"I…" His mouth dropped open. "I did *not*, doctor."

"Brad, I would be honored if you would join our staff in that capacity. The hospital would have to allow you work there under our supervision."

"Wow. I'd be the one feeling honored, Doctor Sewell." He grinned. "Of course I accept. Is there something I need to do?"

"Beside the paperwork? Just promise to pray with us for our sick patients."

TWENTY FOUR

Weeks went by, and there was no response from Brad. Jackie still thought of him every day, of course, but the routine of college was a welcome distraction.

The art studio at Jackie's college was in a loft with high arching, north-facing windows and diffusing skylights. A half dozen students were with her, sitting or standing at their easels, trying to be creative or at least trying to look like they were. Lorne Barnes, their professor, moved from one to the other, offering suggestions.

Professor Barnes stood behind Jackie for awhile before he politely coughed. "You're usually so proficient and inventive, Jackie. What do you have to say about this jumbled mess I see?"

"Oh, Mister Barnes," she turned to face him brush in hand. "You're so right. I'm trying to paint people in motion and I've never tried before. I've blurred the arms and legs but it doesn't look right, does it?"

"The woman with the blonde pigtail—is that you?"

"Yes sir. I slipped on wet grass a few weeks ago and a nice man caught me."

"Well," he chuckled. "It looks like the ground is about to catch you both. I'll tell you what. Put this oil aside and start again with watercolor. That medium might be less forgiving, but it will be easier to show motion. Try a few samples on plain paper."

"Discard the oil completely?"

"Think of it as a crumpled page on an author's floor." He smiled. "Later, when it dries, you can give it a whitewash and reuse it, just like the old masters did."

Jackie tacked up a sheet of paper. "Okay, I'll practice."

"When you want to show an arm in motion, the forward edge should be sharp. The trailing portion—where the arm had been—should be washed out and foreshortened."

"Oh, yes. That makes sense."

"Also, I'd suggest drawing the man so he's coming at us. That way you can show his features more clearly."

"Yeah, thanks--great idea."

The professor picked up a Gesso board from a stack by the wall and leaned it against her easel. "After your practice, make a pencil sketch and show me when you're finished, but first, I want to ask you something."

He motioned for Jackie to follow him toward the window. "I'm told you are teaching art to homeless women down in LA. That's very commendable."

"Thank you, professor. It's a real joy."

Barnes craned his neck and searched the scene below. "I don't see her now but we have one of those very women drifting through our campus."

"A homeless woman?"

"Yes, a girl, really--young and shy. The faculty are concerned for her welfare. She usually sleeps in the bushes next to the science building over there and seems to live off what she finds in the dumpster by the cafeteria."

"Yuck."

"Indeed. She's good at avoiding any of us and the campus police. She may run from you as well, but considering your experience with the homeless, I'd like you to try and make contact with the poor child. If that fails, the police would be our last resort."

"Oh, I hope not. I'll try something that has worked before, but I'll need to borrow a field easel from you and pop up seat, okay?"

"Hey, all yours, Jackie--and good luck."

TWENTY FIVE

Jeffrey Abraham was recovering. Doctor Sewell and Brad stood on one side of bed while the police conducted their interview. One officer took notes on Jeff's age, former address and history before the detective, an older man, began probing for details.

"Mister Abraham, I'm Detective Prado. Your doctor informs me that his X-ray shows you no longer have a left kidney. I assume you have not had any previous operations at that site, correct?"

"Course not--never even been in a hospital before."

"You had Fentenal in your blood stream when you arrived. I'm not here to prosecute you, but it would help us if you honestly told us if you were a user or not."

"Not. I smoke some Mary Janes is all."

"Very well." He turned to the officer to make sure he was writing all this down. "Tell us all you can remember just before you went unconscious."

"Uh—there were a couple of cool dudes—passed me on the street, smoking weed. They said, 'Hey, we're headin' for a joint party. Wanna come?' Said it was put on by a grower, and the joints and music were free—not to mention the girls."

"So you followed them."

117

"Well, natch. Why not, huh?"

"Do you remember where you walked?"

"No walkin', man. This black limo pulls up by my alley. They say that's our ride--but I should a been suspicious, right?"

"Your alley?"

"Yeah, where I usually crash. It's just two blocks from here."

Brad said, "I'll show you later."

The detective acknowledged Brad with a nod. "Jeff, do you recall anything else?"

"Last thing was the needles. This big guy was in the car. He had a fake beard and mustache and pulls out some syringes he calls 'happy starts.' He makes it look like he's shooting up the two guys but I can tell he's not really doing it. Right then I knew something wasn't right."

"Did you try and get away?"

"I hollered 'no,'and grabbed for the door, but we're goin' like sixty miles an hour down Baker Street. My so-called new friends grab me while the heavy one puts the needle in me. Next thing I know it's six days later and I'm lying near the alley again."

The detective shook his head. "I'm really sorry, Jeff. Unfortunately, this sort of thing isn't rare but we'll see if we can't bring these crooks to justice. They get a lot of money for a healthy kidney on the black market."

Jeff frowned at the detective. "Maybe I could at least get ten percent?"

TWENTY SIX

Jackie set up the portable easel on the lawn near a campus path with the Science Building behind her. It was late afternoon and she hoped the girl would pass her on the way to her usual sleeping place. She began working on the final sketch of her action scene.

Almost an hour went by without any sight of her quarry when, out of the corner of her eye, she spied the girl slowly coming across the lawn between buildings. The tall, slender teen wore a dirty, dark blue sweatshirt that hung over torn, faded jeans. Tangled, ash blonde hair hung to her shoulders in clumps.

The girl came to a stop well behind the easel and slipped off her backpack. Jackie kept sketching and pretended not to notice.

The girl took a few hesitant steps toward the artist and watched for awhile as Jackie began adding color. Finally, words came. "He's tryin' to kill her, huh?"

"Nuh-uh." Jackie turned toward the girl and let loose a radiant smile that could have brought a horse to its knees. "She's slipping and about to fall but he caught her."

"You see it happen?"

"Uh huh. That's me in his arms."

The teen scowled. "What did he do next?"

"He, uh… She looked up at the sky, sighed, and her expression became wistful. "He gently put me down on my feet and then he asked me out. So I guess he's my boyfriend now."

"Yeah? How long have you been going out?"

"Well," Jackie chuckled and pondered a moment. "Beginning to end? Eight hours and fifteen minutes."

That got a laugh. "Not really a boyfriend."

Jackie shrugged but held out her hand. "I'm Jackie, by the way."

She didn't take the hand but replied, "I'm Katie, by way of just passing by."

"Do you like my drawing?"

"I could do better."

Jackie let out a squeak and stamped her foot. "What's *wrong* with it?"

"The guys face could use more shading and his mouth looks weak."

"Okay, then," she stood up, moved the seat to one side and held out a pencil for Katie. "If you're so good, I dare you. Draw me a happy girl face."

"Right on your board?"

"Yup, right here on the corner."

"Sure." Katie sat down with a toss of her straggly hair, but with a look of confidence that could have belonged to a queen stepping down from her carriage. She swirled the pencil in the air like a gladiator about to charge. "Watch and learn."

Pencil strokes rapidly moved over the canvas and Katie quietly hummed a tune. She ended with her initials and poke-poke with the pencil before she turned to face her challenger. "What do you think?"

Jackie's beautiful grin smiled back at her. "Katie—wow. God's given you a great gift. You're better than I am, and you're what—seventeen?"

"Thirteen, and I could have done better but I haven't eaten in awhile and my hand's kinda shaky."

"Gosh, girl," She squeezed Katie's shoulder. "Now I'm gonna have to buy you dinner at the cafeteria. It's getting dark. Could you help me lug this stuff over to the Liberal Arts building?"

Katie picked up the easel and chair. "Okay, but I don't think I'm allowed to go where you eat. Besides, I don't look so good right now."

"Nonsense. I'm allowed to bring a guest but," she looked Katie over and pouted. "Yeah, I guess we'll have to wash up first."

TWENTY SEVEN

Brad was glad that Jeff was Sewell's patient since it allowed him to be back in the hospital again. The next morning he was drawing his blood and adjusting the IV. "You're doing just fine, Jeff. Your temperature is almost normal and vital signs are right on the money. How are you feeling?"

"Weak as a wet noodle but I guess I should be glad to be alive."

"How's the pain?"

"The anger or the ouch?"

Brad withdrew the needle, applied a bandage and smiled at his patient. "Both."

"It doesn't hurt when I lie on my right side, but I can't stop thinking how I hate these guys."

"No one would blame you for that. I hope they catch that gang before they attack someone else, but hate's not healthy for your body. We're about to move you out of the ICU into a regular room. If it's okay with you, I'd like to share what I've learned about forgiveness when we get there."

"Yeah? Right now my only comfort is imagining them burning in hell, but knock yourself out."

When they arrived in the private room, a nurse and an aid cranked up the bed and fluffed up Jeff's pillows while Brad fixed the IV to a pole and checked the flow. When they were alone, Brad began with, "Forgiving the ones who've hurt you is hard, but it doesn't mean you have to like them."

"Huh? Why should I even *want* to forgive them?"

"Because continuing to hate is like taking rat poison and waiting for the rat to die."

Jeff looked away and sighed. "Very funny, but I don't think any trick psychology is gonna make it go away."

"Absolutely right. There are a lot of things we can't do on our own, but we can do most anything with God's help."

"Uh oh, don't go preacher man on me, okay?"

Brad smiled. "Nah, I won't push you, but now you have a little time to think about things you might have done differently. Maybe there's something you wish you could wipe out of the record."

Jeff stared at him for a few moments. "Could we talk about something else?

"We could go over the next steps in your care."

"Next? How about that hot nurse's aid comes back in and fluffs my pillows again?"

"Well…" Brad chuckled. "I'm sure she'll be back sometime, but after they pamper you here for a week, you'll go to rehab for a month."

"Then what?"

"Good question. Assuming you're about back to normal, that's up to you. You can either go back on the street, or work on the person you could be—the person God and I know you *can* be. For starters, I know of some Christian men's shelters that specialize in *real* rehabilitation.

"But no weed, huh?"

"No, but they have something way better for you."

TWENTY EIGHT

Jackie and Katie schlepped the equipment over to the Art Room and found the professor locking up the wall cabinets. Jackie said, "Sorry I'm late, Mister Barnes. Thanks for loaning me the chair and easel."

Barnes couldn't conceal his surprise when he turned and saw who was with her. "No, problem. Who's your new assistant?"

"Oh, this is Katie, Mister Barnes. She's an artist, too." Jackie held up the portrait for him to see. "She did this sketch of me in nothing flat."

The professor studied the work for a moment and said, "I'm impressed, Katie. I think you're a child prodigy."

"I'm no child—and what's a prodi-gee?"

He smiled. "My apology. It's a young person with exceptional talent, and I hope you'll apply to Barden College when you're older."

Katie's gaze was on the floor, but she couldn't conceal the grin. Barnes handed the Gesso board back to Jackie. "Put this on the shelf for the next class. I see you've got a fine sense of motion in your figures, now. Good job."

"Thanks, Mister Barnes."

As soon as they stashed the supplies, Jackie put her hand on Katie's shoulder and made eye contact. "Okay, next stop--Ladies Room, girl. Gotta wash up."

Since it was after hours, the rest room was empty. Katie's hands and face required a double scrubbing. Jackie took a comb from her purse and began to work on the girl's hair. "All these leaves in your hairdo, little sister—you trying for the Greek nymph look?"

Katie chuckled but shook her head. "I still don't think I'm ready to be in public."

"Nonsense, you're on a college campus, girl. A few more tears in your jeans and shreds on your shirt and you'll fit right in. Come on. I think you said you were hungry?"

"Yeah? You have no idea, Jackie."

As promised, no one in the cafeteria paid any attention to them. Jackie picked a table by the wall and watched Katie devour her supper—plus a second helping. She waited until they were finishing the lemon meringue pie, before she unleashed one of her special smiles. "So, little sister, what's been going *on* in your life anyway, huh?"

"Ahh," She frowned. "Who cares?"

"I care, and I'm guessing life has blasted you off the road a few times, right?"

"Yeah, but that's over. I'm on my own now and I'm heading south."

Katie's frown began to tremble. Jackie reached over, put her hand on top of hers. She replied just above a whisper. "Katie, most thirteen year old girls are not out on their own and hitchhiking to nowhere."

"Yeah, well," she grimaced. "Most girls don't have a mother who lives in a gin bottle. Even so, I could 'a taken care of mom but she married this creep the day she met him in Vegas. He raped me twice. I tried to fight him off but the second time he hurt me bad, I mean, *real* bad—said he'd kill me if I ever gave him trouble again."

"Uggh. That's just *horrible*, Katie. So you ran away."

Katie shrugged. "No choice."

"I get it, but don't you have any relatives?"

"Just an older brother."

"Couldn't he help?"

"He's deployed in Afghanistan."

"Oh." Jackie shook her head. "Truth is, you might be safer in Afghanistan than out on the street here at night."

"I'll take my chances." She gave a brief look of defiance.

"Say, I'm heading back home near Los Angeles tomorrow. That's the day before Thanksgiving and my roommate already left this morning." Jackie was overcome with compassion as she watched the broken girl stare at her empty plate. "Look, I want you to stay in her bunk tonight and come with me tomorrow, okay?"

"I can make it on my own." Head up, lips smashed tightly together. "Why should I go with you?"

Jackie moved her head close to Katie's. "Cause I'm heading south?"

TWENTY NINE

"All right, Jeff, it's coming up on Thanksgiving and you're all set for rehab. They'll continue with your physical therapy and a social worker will talk about discharge from there. I doubt they'll mention a Christian men's shelter, but Doctor Sewell and I think that's the best option for you."

"So, where's that?"

"I'll do a little research and let you know."

"Ah, I'll be okay out on my own."

Brad made a funny face. "Jeff, you can't spare another kidney."

Jeff chuckled and shook his head. "Point taken, but what's the shelter gonna do for me?"

"You'll get breakfast, dinner and a bunk for the night at least until spring, but most important, you'll get some spiritual guidance."

"So they think they can turn me into Mister Rogers?"

"Nah," Brad shook his head. "Some marines, quarterbacks and even Kanye West love the Lord."

Jeff's finger shot upward. "Oh, I forgot to tell you. A detective came by this morning and said they arrested someone in connection with my attack. They're not finished with the investigation but they might want me to testify in the trial."

"Good. I hope they'll be able to save someone else from what you went through." He gave Jeff a squinty look. "Maybe it'll ratchet your anger down a notch?"

Jeff looked up at the ceiling and let out a breath. "Wanna hear something weird, though? I got to thinking. These guys are still nasty SOBs for what they did, but I just realized something. That kidney of mine—maybe it saved someone else's life."

That made Brad smile. "You know, I think you're right. Can I pray for you?"

Jeff tossed his hand in the air. "Sure."

"Dear Jesus, we thank you for your loving presence in our lives. We thank you that for those who know you, you work all things for the good. I pray that Jeff will open his heart to you, forgive his attackers, and may he abide with you always."

Doctor Sewell came in as he was speaking and said, "Uh oh, they're gonna kick out the preaching PA again."

Jeff said, "Oh no, doc. I told him it was okay."

Sewell gave Jeff's toe a squeeze and chuckled. "Only kidding. How are you feeling today?"

"Like I'm ready to skateboard."

"Great." He gestured for Brad to come with him. "I'll be right back, Jeff."

In the hallway, Sewell said, "I just came from the mailroom. Did you know that once you're off hospital payroll, they destroy any unclaimed mail in ninety days?"

"They have my home address. I assumed they'd forward it."

"No, they're not a post office but the man in charge told me you have a letter in this weeks 'heave-ho' box."

"Probably just another ad, but I'll check it out."

The clerk in the mail room handed him a single letter--a pink one that smelled like a flower. It was from Jacqueline Rogers, postmarked over two months ago. Brad mumbled "Oh, my God" as he tore it open.

Dear Brad:

This is the only address I have for you so I hope you get it. First, I want to apologize for the awful way I brushed you off on Saturday—all my fault. It's some silly protective mechanism of mine that obviously doesn't work, but now I think you cured me.

Brad, you're the nicest guy I've ever met and of course I'd like to see you again. I'll be back in Los Angeles over Thanksgiving so maybe then. If you're still interested in seeing this nutty woman again, write me back or shoot out an Email. If not, turn this note into a paper airplane and try to hit the bucket the first time.

Your friend,

Jackie

PS: I hope you like your portrait.

THIRTY

It took a few tries but finally Jackie had her traveling companion singing along with her favorite CDs on the drive toward LA.

Katie stopped her between songs. "Look, you're a nice lady and all, but why are you doing all this for me? And why are we pulling off the freeway?"

"Nice *lady*? I hope I didn't just go from girl to lady and miss out on all the young woman fun. Katie, you are smart, beautiful and talented." They stopped at a light and Jackie turned to make eye contact. "Did you know there's a book in heaven with your name in it and a 'God plan' for your life—and it's a wonderful life, I'm sure."

Katie looked out the window and sighed. "Awww shish."

"I'm helping you, not just because I like you, and I do, but because I've discovered that nothing makes me happier than working with God to help with His amazing plans."

"Yeah, well what's that so-called plan got to do with this shopping center you just pulled into? We ate two hours ago."

"God has sent us," she giggled, "to Kohl's to equip you for His kingdom plan."

Katie laughed. "Oh, shoot. You really are a kook. So, now you're spending your own money to buy me clothes?"

"No way. I'm putting it on daddy's 'only-for-emergency' credit card."

That got Katie doubled over in laughter. "Well, *thank* you, Sugar Daddy."

Two of the outfits were a bit conservative for Katie's taste, but she relented. For her part, Jackie allowed Katie one pair of shorts and a T-shirt--at least the shirt read "John 3:16."

Back on the road again, Jackie said, "Katie, I'm curious. Why did you pick our college to escape from Rolf?"

Katie gazed out the window before she answered. "I couldn't go to my friends houses. Their parents would only call my house and tell them where I am. I tried a park, but there were creepy men around—and there was that car."

"You found a car to sleep in?"

"No, there was a man and a woman who kept following me around and trying to get me in. The lady would sound real sweet, you know. She'd say, 'You need a safe place to stay, darling. We'll take care of you—we promise.' They told us all about that game in school."

"Human traffickers."

"No question, but they were real persistent—almost grabbed me when I put down to sleep once. Then I saw your campus police patrolling twenty four hours. I had to avoid them too, of course, but I figured the bad guys wouldn't follow me in there."

"Good thinking, girl." Jackie craned her neck to get a quick eye contact. "I had your protection in mind when I insisted on cover up clothes, little sister. Your good looks are actually a problem for you. You'll have enough trouble in the days ahead without every man after you."

"Not to worry *big sister,*" she chuckled. "Right now I hate all men."

Jackie shot her a grin. "Might be best for now, but *all* men are not bad guys. We women just have to figure out who's who. Look, I'm no genius on that score. I just blew off a real peach and I'm hurting."

"Oh, sorry." Concern came into Katie's tone. "Isn't there some way you can make it up to him?"

"I wrote him a nice note two months ago—even included a portrait sketch of him, but he never answered. So, like you found out, sometimes you just gotta move on."

"Bummer." Katie wiggled around. "This big bra itches me in the back."

"Probably the label. I'll cut it off next rest stop. Actually, we're less than an hour away now."

"Don't get me wrong, Jackie. I really appreciate the new duds, but oh yeah--you never said what your," she chuckled, "I mean, what's *God's* plan for me next."

"Right." She raised a finger. "I confess I don't have the answer, but I think the first stop will be the women's shelter where I volunteer. It's run by Martha Eldridge and she'll have a better idea about that 'what's next' thing. I'd guess the ultimate plan will be for you to hook up with a Christian foster home."

"Uh oh, a friend told me that Child Services only sends you right back to the bio-mom. I'll slit my throat first."

"Easy there." Jackie waved her hand. "That won't happen, Chickie. I know Martha works with the courts and she's got a bunch of pro bono lawyers. Once your home is declared unfit, you're eligible for foster care, and I heard our new president took away the regulations blocking Christian agencies."

"Humph." Katie went back to staring at the passing scenery. "Can't imagine a father who'd actually be nice to me."

"You already have a perfect Father in *heaven* who loves you. Maybe we can find you a human father who lives by His word."

Katie looked down and shook her head. "Sounds like a fairy tale. I don't think I could ever trust another man."

"Yeah, well the people are supposed to be checked out beforehand, and besides, any family who gets you will have to pass my test too, so leave your carving knife in the drawer."

THIRTY ONE

Brad pulled out of the used car lot, the proud owner of a Ford Fusion that sported a hideous green repaint job and ninety thousand miles of experience. The car salesman told him it was such a good buy 'cause hybrids get good mileage and run forever, but when the smaller battery died on the first day, he was beginning to think his luck with cars paralleled his luck with women. However, Brad had a brilliant idea, sheer genius, he thought.

The evening before Thanksgiving Brad eased his green slug into a parking space at Saving Grace church and marched up to the shelter office, clip board in hand. He felt the board would give him an "all business, how could you doubt me," look.

The door to the office was open and the director sat to one side of her desk typing on a computer. A large, black dog sat in the middle of the floor looking at him with a quizzical stare. Brad rapped on the doorframe. "Uh, Mrs. Eldridge, could I have a moment of your time?"

She peered at him over her glasses. "And who are you?"

"Brad McKinley, M'am. Maybe you remember me from the bounce house at the church fair." He reached out to pet the dog but he was met with a growl. "Oops, he doesn't like me."

"Keeper's telling me you're anxious. How can I help you?"

"He's right. I am. First off, I'm wondering if you have a list of men's Christian rehabs in the general vicinity? I have a patient I'm trying to place." She studied him for a moment through squinted eyes. "Have a seat by that table, won't you. I'll be with you in a minute." Martha resumed her computer work.

Brad sat, but his eyes wandered about the room. Suddenly, he noticed a row of wall photos. He slipped over to study them: kitchen staff with a cafeteria background, recreation staff with a field background and English Education in a classroom. Wait, there it was: the art staff surrounded by sculptures and paintings. And there *she* was, standing with another staff member behind a cadre of students.

He leaned in close to read the caption. "Jacqueline Rogers, art instructor."

He turned around when he heard an "Ahem." Martha was holding out a folder in her hand so he approached the desk and took it. She said, "Here are all the Christian men's rehabs in the county. If you have a medical patient I'd recommend Twin Oaks. They have a full time RN on staff."

Brad glanced at the folder and put it down quickly. "Martha, there's something else--real important." Keeper growled again, now from behind the desk.

She was standing and opened her hands in a "Well?" gesture.

"Look, I'll be frank. I'm trying to get in touch with Jackie. It's really important to me, but I don't have her phone number, Email or local address. I know she volunteers here so I thought you might…"

"Hold it, Brad." Martha flashed the stop signal with one hand. "You know I can't give out that information for security and privacy reasons."

"Oh, *please,* this is different. She'd want to hear from me. I know she would." Keeper barked twice.

"Well, that may be true, but rules are rules." Martha smiled.

"Oh, so you think this is funny. Look, can't you make an exception? You *know* I'm not a bad guy."

"Okay, okay, I can think on one way you *might* get the information—just might, I mean."

"Martha, whatever it is, I'll do it."

Her smile turned into a grin. "You could turn around and ask her for yourself."

Eyes pop open—quick spin around. There was Jackie picking out supplies from a shelf by the door and trying really hard to look nonchalant. "Jackie!"

"Oh, hello, Brad," came the demure reply.

He took two quick steps toward her. "Oh, God, Jackie, you must be furious with me, but honest, I only opened your letter this *morning.*"

"Cause you tossed it aside?"

"No, no, because I was fired from Los Angeles General for praying with patients. No one told me I had a letter in the mail room until today."

"What? You *really* just got it?"

"Yes." He grasped both her shoulders, and she smiled. "But, but, Jackie, I've been thinking about you *every* single day. I've been wanting to see you so bad."

Martha was seated, watching with a grin, her head resting on her hand, "No kissing in my office," she said. They kissed. "Well, maybe just this *once*."

Jackie laughed and wiped the lipstick off his lip with her sleeve. "They fired you for *praying?*"

"Hard to believe, I know, but Doctor Sewell hired me and I'll complete my internship with him." His left hand cupped the side of her face while his thumb stroked her cheek.

"Well, I'm still angry with you," she said with a pout. "You're going to have to take me out to dinner to make it up."

Martha continued to soak in the action, her face locked in a grin. When they kissed again, she chuckled. "Okay *twice*, but that's it you two."

THIRTY TWO

Jackie released Brad and turned to Martha. "Oh, sorry, I forgot where we were."

Martha, whose head still rested on her hand, looked up. "No problem. This is better than NetFlicks, but don't forget to check in on our new guest before you leave."

"I was planning to. Is it okay if I show Brad around? Our main doors are still closed so there's no other ladies around."

'Sure." Martha sat back and tilted her head. "I think he'll follow you anywhere."

Jackie giggled and began piling art supplies in his arms. "Help me with this stuff and we can make it in one trip."

As they left the office, Martha called after them, "God bless you both."

In the Art Room they unloaded their cargo and wrote down each other's phone numbers and addresses. "Say, Jackie," Brad asked, "Are you teaching a class today, or should I pick you up at your folks place?"

"I don't have a class until the day after Thanksgiving, so could you come for me at my house about six?"

"Love to."

"Great," she took his hand and pulled him out the door. "Come on, I'll show you our facility."

After touring the activity rooms, kitchen and dining hall, they ran into a woman who walked briskly down a hall with a folder clutched to her chest and a look of intensity on her face. Jackie said, "Hi, Gina, how's it going?"

Gina slammed to a halt and studied the pair. "Well look at that. How long have you two been back together?"

Jackie giggled. "About forty minutes. Did you finish your first course toward a teacher's certificate?"

"Yup. One down and three to go. I can't wait to start sending out applications." She smiled at Brad. "Did she send you a portrait?"

Jackie winced, but Brad grinned. "Sure did and it's really professional. I just wish she had a better looking subject."

"Ah, don't be modest." Gina pointed a finger at Jackie. "I'll expect a full report later. Life is pretty dull here." She laughed.

Jackie glanced up at Brad. "Hard to believe, but Gina used to be deeply depressed."

"Really?" He looked at Gina. "What would you like to teach, Gina?"

"Biology and Earth Science, but I can teach some other subjects too."

"Hey, great. They're pre-med. I took both of them. Well, I wish you the best of luck—uh, if you don't mind, what happened to your depression?"

141

Gina pointed her finger at Jackie and chuckled. "She's what happened to it. No one can stay depressed around her."

Jackie shook her head. "Not true. It was discovering the Lord's love and forgiveness."

"Not to mention getting excited about my future again, but you led me there, dear one, and wait until my class learns that life's diversity didn't come just from evolution."

"Watching you come out of that thing was my absolute pleasure, Gina. So, you don't feel like you're walking on a tight rope anymore, huh?"

She grinned. "I'm walking a solid path with my Savior by my side."

Brad lifted an arm straight up. "Halleluiah! That's beautiful, Gina. So glad to meet you. I'll be stopping by again."

"Yeah, I'm guessing you will. Okay," She schussed them away with the back of her hand. "Gotta get back to work on the computer. Glad to meet you too, Brad."

The last stop was the large sleeping hall in a converted basketball court. It was empty save for Katie who sat on a bed against one wall playing a game on her cell phone.

As they approached, Jackie asked, "You have a cell phone?"

Katie looked up, gave Brad a suspicious look, and responded. "Martha gave me a temporary one. She said it was for security until—well I guess until she figures out what to do with me."

Jackie smiled. "Oh, good. Katie, this is my friend Brad. He's one of the good guys I told you about."

"Uh huh."

"You'll find there *are* some men you can trust. He's one of them."

Katie looked up at him with a frown. "So, he's the one you kept boo-hooing about cause he never wrote you back?"

Jackie and Brad laughed. "Yes, but it turned out he had a very good reason—and it's none of your business." Jackie put hands on hips. "So, here's where you'll be living for a few days. In a couple of hours a whole bunch of adult women will be coming in to claim their beds for the night. You'll all get dinner at six, a brief message from a local pastor, and then you're on your own."

"Oh, good. I saw a bar down the street." Jackie let out a horrified squeak.

Katie grinned and finger-pointed. "Gotcha."

Jackie pouted, shook her head and chuckled. "You did. Got any *real* questions?"

"Any TV here?"

"Oh, yes, I forgot. It's in the cafeteria, but our ladies usually vote for Hallmark movies and news."

"So, no MTV, huh?"

"Well," she smirked. "You might tell them you're Martha's VIP and you get to pick whatever you want after their movie."

Katie rolled her eyes, but Jackie continued. "Listen, tomorrow is Thanksgiving. There will be a special dinner a little earlier than usual and some live entertainment afterwards. Make some friends while you're here. I think you'll have a good time."

"Yeah, I know. I'm gonna be stuck with a bunch of old ladies, right?"

"No, some aren't real old. Some are my age, but here's another choice for you. I spoke with my parents and they'd be delighted if you would join us for Thanksgiving--but don't feel you have to."

Katie wasn't making eye contact but answered. "Sure, I guess."

"Great. It's settled, then." Jackie made a few dance moves until Katie looked at her. Big Jackie grin. "Super. I'll come by for you at four thirty tomorrow, and if it helps to make your mind up, my mom's dinner will be even 'special-er' than this one."

THIRTY THREE

That evening, Jackie and Brad were exchanging silly grins and lengthy eye-locks while munching egg rolls at Tangs Taipei Wok. After catching up on Brad's life as a PA intern and Jackie's hopes and aspirations, she tossed him a question. "Brad, you'll be spending Thanksgiving tomorrow with your family, right?"

"Normally I would, but my Dad's a pastor, and this year he's getting some rest before the Christmas rush." Brad dipped one of those curly things into their shared sweet and sour sauce. "My folks are in Honolulu at a beach hotel for retired military."

"Really? Gosh, I hope you don't have to work tomorrow."

Brad munched on his appetizer, pursed his lips and looked up, feigning deep thought. "Not exactly. I'm on call from eleven tonight to seven AM. After a little sleep catch up, I'll be eating a large turkey sandwich at Bailey's pub before I watch Gilligan's Island reruns in my apartment."

Jackie laughed, grabbed his forearm then slapped it. "You most certainly will *not*, mister. You are joining us for Thanksgiving dinner and I won't listen to any excuses."

"You know I'd love to, but wouldn't that make two people you've added to your parent's dinner without asking them."

"Are you kidding? My mom *lives* for this sort of thing."

"And, your dad?"

"Oh," She pointed a finger at him and laughed. "Get ready. He'll be checking you out against his list of qualifications."

THIRTY FOUR

Brad was cleaning up after a late breakfast in his apartment Thanksgiving morning when his phone rang.

"OMG Brad, Katie's gone!"

"Gone? You mean she went on a walk somewhere?"

"No, I mean really gone. I'm here at Saving Grace. They said she took some food from the kitchen and left with all her things."

"Didn't anyone see which way she went?"

"Our homeless women come and go all the time. No one in our sleeping area paid any attention."

"I wouldn't worry. I'll bet she just wants some alone time."

"Please come over and help me look for her." Jackie's voice cracked. *"I'm really upset."*

"Hang on. I'll be right there."

Jackie was waiting for him in the foyer, pacing the floor in distress. "Brad, thanks for coming. Martha sent out four women in different directions and they all came back empty. Katie's very unstable. There's no telling what she might do and the police won't even call her missing for twenty four hours."

"All right, let's be calm. We need to have a plan."

"I took a jog around the block." She shook her head. "Brad, I looked in the garden and checked her bed for clues. *Nothing!*"

"Okay, okay." Brad took her hand and sat her down on a bench. "Let's think positive. We're *going* to find this little lady. God's on our side." She bit her lip and frowned. "What's the first thing we need to do, Jackie?"

Her eyes flashed open. "Oh, pray."

"Right." He took both her hands in his. "Dearest Lord, we come to you as your loving servants and ask for your wisdom and direction. We know how much you love Katie and it is your will she will be found and saved into the Kingdom. We ask for your Holy Spirit to protect her and guide us in our search, in Jesus name. Amen."

"Amen." Jackie squeezed his hands. "Right on, Brad."

Brad gave a quick squeeze back and released his grip. "Okay, let's try and think like she would. Where did she hang out on your campus?"

"She wandered, but she had a favorite sleeping place beside a building, hidden behind some bushes. I looked in our garden, but she's not there."

"Okay, unless she got on a bus, she's likely in a park or garden. But for Plan A, I'll contact a man I know who can locate her cell phone."

"I already know how to locate it."

"Great. Your facility has access to that program?"

"No, she left it on her pillow."

Brad crossed his eyes and stuck out his tongue. "Moving on to plan B—we get a map and start checking parks and companies with landscaping."

"Ah ha. There's free city guide maps right by the door." She pointed, "and I know where there's a park five blocks away, but I'm thinking she might go to the art museum. It's not too far, but it's the other way."

Brad picked up a map. "I'll bet Katie took one of these on her way out. Do you want to take a sweater? It's kinda chilly."

"Nah, I'm fine. Let's get hiking."

The pair began literally beating the bushes. Brad even climbed a wall into a locked up church for a look around. When they came to a main avenue there was a sign for the city park. They asked a few homeless men along the way and a man trimming bushes on the edge of the park. No luck.

They cris-crossed through all the foot paths in the park and checked all the bushes along the way. Finally, Jackie sighed and rested her head on Brad's shoulder. "Where to next, Brad? The art museum? The bus depot?"

"I'm not done here yet, darlin'." With squinted eyes he meticulously turned and studied the area. "Wait. Look at that statue of Balboa. I don't think it goes against the wall behind it—in fact I can see some shrubbery back there."

They started jogging toward it. Jackie saw a flash of red that came and went. She grabbed his arm. "Brad, I bought her a red cap at Kohl's."

They climbed up on the base of the statue and saw it was four feet from the perimeter wall with bushes in between. Peering down, Jackie spotted two feet wearing the pink tennis shoes she bought earlier peeking out from a bush. "Praise the Lord," she murmured.

The two slid down to the ground on either side expecting their quarry to bolt. Katie jerked her feet back when she saw them but remained sitting against the wall. She had her back pack opened and possessions were strewn around. "You guys found me pretty quick. Did ya plant a tracer on me?"

Brad sat on the statue base, but Jackie eased in and sat next to her under the leafy canopy. "Nah, the Lord led us to you."

Brad looked down at the pair, offering a comforting smile.

Suddenly, Jackie began sobbing and leaned her head on Katie's shoulder. Katie put a hand on her head and said, "Hey, what's the matter with you. I wasn't gonna commit suicide or nothing."

Jackie looked at her, wet eyes peering through a tortured face. She croaked, "We are *not* going to lose you, Katie. I lost one foster sister and I'm not gonna let that happen again--*ever*."

Neither one had any more words, but Jackie's sobs continued. Brad slipped down beside them, found a tissue for

Jackie's cheeks, took off his jacket, and spread it over both women. Finally, Katie whispered. "But I'm afraid of all those government people. They're gonna come and tell me what I have-ta do."

Jackie shook her head. "No! No. you and I—we're gonna tell *them* what to do."

Katie was on the verge of tears. She croaked, "I hardly know you. Why are you being so good to me, Jackie?"

Jackie's expression drifted into a thin smile and she sighed. "Cause I care about you. Already, I feel like your older sister--one who has loved you for a lifetime."

A tear ran down Katie's cheek and dripped off her pained smile. "I kinda feel it too, but tell me this." She blew out a big breath and pointed a finger at both of them. "Truth time—are you guys gonna call child services on me or not?"

"Truth--" Jackie's look was determined. "The truth is we are on your side and our goal is to find you a Christian foster care home. I want one close enough so we can get together, too, but as I said, Martha is going to have a sit down with you after she makes some calls and does some research."

"But still, the law says you gotta call them, right?"

"I think what will happen is our *lawyers* will call them with proof that your home situation is unsafe."

"But, you don't really know."

"True, but I trust Martha and I know she'll figure out a plan."

"So, it's lawyers, plans, and government."

"No!" Jackie shook her head with gusto. "First it's *God*, Katie, and it's us—all of us. We'll be praying for you and working hard to make sure everything works out right."

Brad said, "I'm on your side too, I promise."

Katie studied the ground. "I think I just wanted to be alone for awhile." She looked up at Brad. "But I guess I'd rather be with you guys." She began to gather up her things.

Jackie helped but paused when she found a photo lying on the ground. "Last thing I'd expect you to have is a man's picture. Who is this handsome, young guy?"

Katie gently took the picture from her, bit her lip and slid it into her jeans pocket. "He's my dad--my real one."

Brad grinned. Okay, here's some good news, Katie. You and me--we just got invited to a great Thanksgiving dinner we thought we wouldn't have."

THIRTY FIVE

Brad wasn't due for a couple of hours so it was time for Jackie to get her "sister" into the best of the clothes she bought and change her black fingernails to pink—well maybe mauve. Katie's sandy blonde hair was the real problem, but after two shampoos and a shorter cut, Jackie had it glistening and swept to one side—a work of art.

Two big grins greeted them in the mirror. Katie pursed her lips. "Gosh it looks like I've been to a salon. How'd you learn to do that?"

"Night school course--my plan B in case no one wants to hire an art teacher."

Katie chuckled. "I look like I'm ready for a prom date."

"You'll have your pick of those when the time comes. You're one beautiful girl, but let's get going. I want to introduce you to my parents before I shock them with Brad."

Katie shot her a look of surprise. "What? They've never met him? They don't even know he's coming?"

Jackie showed gritted teeth and crossed her eyes. "Uh, nope."

"But you *must* have told them all about him—uh, right?"

"Uh, double nope. They didn't even hear his name 'til I casually dropped it yesterday."

"Oh, gosh." Katie snort laughed. "And you're the genius I'm trusting to dance me into this so-called new life?"

Jackie bit her lip with a "that's-the-way-it-goes" gesture.

Katie returned a smirky, "you-screwed-up" expression. "Okay, sister, I'm going to *pretend* I don't hate all men for awhile and tell them what a great guy Brad is. I'll even tell them he's the one who saved me from my walkabout."

Jackie released her special smile. "Cause it's your turn to save me now?"

"You might be past saving, but let's get rolling. We should help in the kitchen."

*   *   *

Jackie arrived with the all-cleaned-up Katie and introduced her to her parents, Helen and Jim Rogers. Helen promptly gave her a hug. "We're simply delighted to have you join us, Katie."

Jim noted Katie's surprised look at the hug so he opted for, "We were afraid it'd be just the three of us, so it's really great to have Thanksgiving company." He gestured for to come in. "I hear you're an artist?"

Katie coughed and said, "Uh, yeah, I guess. Sorry I didn't bring a bottle of wine or something."

Helen gave her a quirky grin. "And how would you be buying *that*, my dear?"

"I well, right, I—ain't I supposed to…"

"Oh, nonsense." Helen gave her a another quick hug. "Just messing with you, dear one. Come on in and have a seat."

"Uh, couldn't I help you in the kitchen?"

"Why thank you. That's better yet," she chuckled. "Let's set a good example for this lazy daughter of ours." Katie caught a glimpse of Jackie sticking her tongue out and rolling her eyes. She laughed.

Helen put Katie to work mashing potatoes and keeping the gravy stirred and sent her daughter out to pour the sparkling apple cider and fill the water glasses.

Jackie tried to sound casual as she tossed off, "I'll set another place for Brad in case he comes."

"I'm sure he will, dear. We're expecting him."

Jackie hastened into the dining room without responding, but thought, *One day mom has to tell me how to get that sixth sense.*

Helen gave her helper a sweet smile. "Katie, just know that you are so welcome here. We want you to feel comfortable as though this were your home."

She responded with a nod and a weak smile.

Pointing at the gravy, "Turn that down to simmer, would you." She took the covered dish of carrots from the microwave and added, "The peas are cooked, but put some butter on them. We'll zap them again just before we eat."

Meanwhile, by the dinner table, Jim was "supervising."

"Jackie, when was the last time you brought a boyfriend over?"

"Two years ago, and he dumped me the next day, so maybe this time you could avoid giving Brad a full inquisition about how he was going to support me, huh, dad?"

"Oh, I remember that boy. He wasn't right for you anyway, but I hope that's not why we haven't seen any of your men friends since then, is it?"

"No, it's because I haven't *had* any men friends since."

"Really? As charming as you are?"

"I'm working toward a career, Dad, and getting burned again is something I've tried to avoid. I'd pushed the whole idea of involvement to the back of my mind."

"But, along came Brad?"

Cue the magic smile. "Yeah, he's a whole new concept—so be nice, okay?"

Later, when the doorbell rang, Jackie let her father answer it. "Hello, I'm Jim Rogers. You must be Jackie's friend."

"Yes, I…"

Jackie literally skipped over, hugged his shoulders and gave him a cheek kiss. "Yes, he is Jackie's friend." She giggled and both men chuckled.

Jim said, "Welcome to our crazy family gathering."

Jackie tugged on his hand. "Come on, Brad, Dad can talk to you after dinner. Mom's in the kitchen with Katie."

Nancy gave him the traditional mom greeting, wiping her hands on her apron, picking up his hands and nodding with a smile. "Happy Thanksgiving and welcome to our home."

"So glad to be here, Mrs. Rogers. Is there anything I can do to help?"

You and Jim are on turkey carving duty. We're about ready to eat."

Plates full and everyone seated, Jim announced, "I just got a Holy Spirit download. This feels like a special occasion well beyond Thanksgiving. Let's join hands for grace."

Katie was glad she only had to hold hands with Jackie and Nancy. Her worried glance flitted from person to person.

Jim began in a low and forceful voice. "Dear heavenly Father, we are so grateful today for all your gifts and we give thanks for this abundant food, your presence in our lives and the purpose you have given each of us in your glorious kingdom. We dedicate these blessings and our lives to your purpose. Amen."

As they began to eat, Nancy said, "And I give thanks for Jim keeping it short. He likes to give sermons."

Brad said, "My dad is a pastor so anything short of five minutes is short for me."

Jim gave him a finger point." He'd be welcome here. Our family dinners have two rules: no talking politics, but discussing God is required."

After a few bites, Katie leaned toward Jackie and whispered, "This is *so* yummy, Jackie. Thanks."

She smiled. "I love it that you're here with us, but most turkey's taste pretty much the same, don't you think?"

"The only had the frozen dinner kind before. This is way better." Katie pointed to a serving bowl. "What's that brown stuff everyone is having?"

Nancy responded, "Its walnut stuffing, dear. Try some with gravy."

Katie took a bite and her eyebrows went up. "Wow, that's a *lot* better than it looks." Chuckles around the table.

After dinner Brad brought his plate into the kitchen and thanked Nancy for a wonderful meal. Jim put a hand on his shoulder and said, "That's all the duties we old fashioned men have. Let's relax on the back porch while the ladies enjoy their chatter."

Jim pointed to two comfortable outdoor chairs facing a private backyard. He settled into one with a grunt and took a curved pipe out of his pocket. "Mom doesn't let me smoke in the house. Care for some port or brandy, Brad?"

"No, I'm good, thanks. Say that wasn't a test, was it?"

Jim laughed as he packed tobacco in the pipe bowl. "Nah, I don't have to give you a test. It's perfectly obvious you're a decent sort. As a pastor's son, I assume you're a Christian?"

"An imperfect one, but trying to get better."

A cloud of blue smoke emanated from the pipe. "Aren't we all? Look, it's also obvious that you and Jackie are very fond of each other so I feel there's something you should know."

"Oh, oh."

"No, no, here's the thing. You already know that Jackie's the sweetest, most caring woman on the planet and her joy is simply contagious. What you might not realize is she's emotionally fragile. When her dog died a few years ago, her grief was unbearable and she doesn't want to own another one. She even cries when she sees a roadside kill.   Jackie had a boyfriend a couple of years back—really not a person you could get excited about—trust me, but after they broke up, she's avoided relationships ever since."

"I understand." He ducked the smoke cloud heading his way. "It's a normal reaction, but I understand Jackie's a bit more sensitive than most."

"A lot more." Jim put his pipe down, leaned in closer a spoke in a low voice. "Perhaps I shouldn't have said anything, but as a father who loves his daughter I just wanted to speak up. Actually, I think she's ready to take more emotional risk now."

"Jim, while we're being frank, let me say that if something happened to break us apart, I would be the one who'd be an emotional basket case. I want to be like a rock for her—one she can always trust."

Jim chuckled. "Oh, good. You look like a great couple to me. One other thing—and it's something that shows me Jackie's getting tougher—Nancy and I fostered two children. One was a boy who was nine when we got him. Marty went on to college and is engaged to be married. We're proud of him and we keep in touch. The other one was a fourteen year old girl, almost the same age as Jackie was at the time."

"Oh, yeah, Jackie mentioned her today."

Jim renewed his puffing. "This girl, Julie, had a real hard life, but we thought we had her turned around. Jackie took to her like the sister she never had, but when Julie aged out of the foster program at eighteen, she returned to drugs and worse. Julie died of an overdose a year ago and I think Jackie took it as a personal failure."

Brad blew away some smoke. "But I think she relates to Katie as an older sister without any reservation. There's already a strong bond between them."

"You've got some insight, son. Maybe this is the coming change I was feeling at dinner."

"I hope you're right, but I wish I could feel confident about Katie's future."

THIRTY SIX

When the men finished their talk, Brad headed back into the kitchen where the women were finishing up. "Oh, good. I missed all the work."

Jackie shot him a pout and handed him the Cinch and a paper towel. "Not quite, mister. Make these counters sparkle."

Jim put on a football game on in the family room while Nancy had a private chat with Katie. Jackie took hold of Brad's hand and led him outside. "Come on. Before it gets dark I want to show you around my neighborhood."

The streets of their suburb were broad and lined with tall Washingtonian palms. As they walked along, the town was almost deserted, this being a holiday. Jackie pointed out a vacant, grass filled lot where a house burned some years ago. All that remained was an elaborate tree house in the back yard. "The family moved to Texas after it happened but the neighborhood kids all use the house. They call it 'The Hawk's nest.'".

When they reached a bridge spanning a creek, Jackie grabbed his hand and pulled him down a narrow dirt road that followed the brook. "Oh, I gotta show you this." Her hand grabbing thing might be a girlie leftover, but Brad loved it.

She led him to a pond and stepped up onto an arching foot bridge that spanned the stream. Still gripping his hand, Jackie looked up at him. "I wanted to show you one of the pretty places I painted."

Brad glanced over the scene. "Yeah, I remember seeing this painting in your parent's dining room."

She leaned on the guard rail gazing over the pond and the stream bed below. Without facing him she let out a deep breath. "I guess my dad told you about my flaws, huh?"

"Uh huh—but the good things too—lots of them."

"He believes in truth in packaging, like he describes a stock to a potential buyer."

"That sounds a bit harsh. I just think your dad doesn't want to see you hurt."

Jackie turned toward him with a look of intensity. "Tell me straight up. What did he say was my flaw?"

Brad allowed himself a few moments to enjoy gazing into her expectant face. "Basically, your dad said you are vulnerable because you love with reckless intensity, but Jackie, I think you share that trait with God Himself."

"The way you say it--it sounds so sweet." Her face squinched up. "But I think I'm getting vulnerable again."

Brad gently put his hands around her waist. "Not on my watch, sweetheart."

After a lingering smooch, they relaxed. Brad stood, just holding her, enjoying their closeness as she rested her head on his chest.

She spoke in a quiet voice. "I don't have to go back to school until Sunday afternoon. What do you want to do?"

"Well, tomorrow I have to work." He grinned. "So I'm giving you a day to miss me, but we can spend all day Saturday together. I thought you might like to go downtown and see the art museum. The traveling exhibit of Egyptian antiquities came in and there are great restaurants everywhere."

She gave him the doe eyed grin. "I do have to teach my art class in the morning, but after that, I'm all yours. Should I assume you'll be taking me to church Sunday?"

"Of course." They embraced cheek to cheek. Brad whispered. "Others might say I haven't known you long enough to have anything more than a crush." He cupped her cheek in his hand. "But, Jackie, I feel like I've loved you forever."

THIRTY SEVEN

As they bounced through the front door, Jackie was giggling about something Brad had said. Jim sat close to the TV watching a game with the volume turned down. They approached Nancy and Katie who sat beside each other on a nearby couch. Jackie asked, "Whatcha talking about, mom?"

Nancy looked up with a gentle smile. "Oh, Katie and I were just having a chat. She certainly has been through a lot of terrible things."

"I'll say. Her last home situation was pure poison" Jackie sat down cross-legged on the rug in front of them while Brad drifted over to join Jim and the game.

Katie shook her head. "But, like I said, my mom and I were working things out before 'Frankenstein' moved in. Back then I was helping her get off the booze and she'd agreed to go to AA. We even had beach days once in awhile and sometimes I was allowed to have Meg and our friends over."

Nancy's eyebrows lowered. "Katie, dear, did you ever call your mom and tell her you are all right?"

"No." Katie shook her head with vigor. "I can't let *anyone* know where I am, and besides, *he* might answer."

"Katie," Jackie opened her hands. "You're safe here, but I know what. We'll call on my dad's business cell phone. It has a Saint Louis area code and, hey, Brad will even make the call so you won't have to talk to that man no matter what."

Nancy nodded. "Yes, and what a wonderful Thanksgiving gift that would be for her. Speaking as a mother, I'd be in agony not knowing where you are."

Katie shrugged her shoulders. Jackie said, "Great," and in a minute she was back with the phone in one hand and pulling wide-eyed, confused Brad with the other. They explained the plan. With the phone on speaker, Brad would ask her mom to go to a private place when she answered.

There were many rings before a croaky voice said, *Hello?*

"This is Bradford McKinley from the Los Angeles Hospital. Is this Mrs. Rita Sanderson?"

Yes, what is it?

"I have some information regarding your daughter Katherine but it is important that you go to a private location so I can tell you in confidence."

My, God, you know where she is? Is Katie all right?

"Are you by yourself, Mrs. Sanderson?"

My husband is out partying with his friends. What do you know about Katie?

Brad smiled and handed her the phone. "Hi, mom. Happy Thanksgiving."

Katie! She had a coughing spell. *My God—you're okay? Where are you?*

"I'm fine, mom. I'm with some friends in the Los Angeles area. I don't want to say exactly where 'cause he might come after me."

Oh, thank God. I'm so relieved to know you're okay and I understand why you left. (cough) *Rolf is totally out of control and it's dangerous for you here. Just tell me you found a safe place. You're not sleeping outside somewhere, are you?*

"No, my friends got me off the street. They're Christians and they're trying to set me up with something permanent. You're not gonna file papers to get me back, are you?"

Oh, no. She had a long coughing spell and her voice was strained. *Tell your brother John if you can reach him overseas.*

"Ma, you don't sound good."

Yeah, I've been real sick, and Rolf won't take me to the doctor. You'll be glad to know I haven't had a drink in a week, though.

"Good going, ma. Look, if you're not better, take a cab to the doctor, huh?"

Okay. I better get back in bed. I love you.

"I love you too, ma. I'll call again, okay?"

Bless you. Bye now.

The chorus of yeas and thumbs up surrounding Katie made her smile. They spent some time talking about her old life and prospects for the new one. Nancy said "This might be the first divorce I could agree to. When does your brother get back from overseas?"

"I think it's in three months. Yeah, maybe John could talk to her about that—meanwhile I'll hang out at the shelter."

Nancy made it clear she wanted Katie to spend Sundays at her home—the excuse being she could use some help. For starters, she and Katie put up bird feeders under floodlights in the dark backyard, folded laundry, and laughed at family photos in an album.

Jackie interrupted them. "I hate to break this up, you two, but our security puts the center on lockdown at eight o'clock."

Brad and Jackie exchanged looks of amazement when Katie gave both her parents a prolonged hug goodbye with tearful thanks. It had been a Thanksgiving Day.

THIRTY EIGHT

With the holiday past, Brad was in Dr. Sewell's work room, toying with his lunch and missing Jackie terribly. He wouldn't see her until his free weekend two weeks from now. Still, life goes on, and he planned to visit Jeff in his rehab after work.

The Life Savers Rehabilitation facility was a sprawling single story complex outside of the city. The large cross over the front door left no doubt about its Christian mission. Brad located Jeff in the activity room tapping away on a computer. "Hi, Jeff. It looks like you are way ahead of yourself in the recovery plan."

"Hey..." He made a few more pokes at the keyboard. "There."

"All your enzymes are normal, even the creatinine. That measures kidney function."

Jeff turned and smiled up at him. "Just so you know, Nurse Thompson is taking all the credit. She says it was her prayers."

"Is that so?" He chuckled. "Don't tell her how many were praying with her."

"The pastor here walked me through a salvation prayer. Does that make me an official, badge wearing Christian?"

"If you've given Jesus your heart and soul, it's way better than a label. You're forever saved, and a child of God."

"Great, so I don't have to take orders from anyone else."

Brad laughed. "Nice try, but God requires us to submit to authority, and that includes your doctor's orders."

"I figured. Say, I've got a job interview next week. It's for a waiter job but they'll watch me bus tables first."

"Way to go, Jeff. I think you'll be up to it physically too. Remember, Dr Sewell wants you to start walking and getting regular exercise every day."

"Sounds boring, but okay."

"Well, how about we make it less boring. Lets you and I spend tomorrow morning walking through a homeless camp. I'm off until noon. There's one below a freeway overpass just blocks from here. I want to pass out some supplies and we'll see what else we can do for them."

With Dr Sewell's orders in the chart, Brad was able to sign Jeff out the next day. They parked off the freeway and Brad gave Jeff a shoulder bag like his. They headed down the bank on a path worn through the weeds, slipped under a hole cut in the fence and approached a dozen camper tents.

Brad said, "You've got water bottles in your bag to give out and in the outside pocket there's a pad and pencil. Write down the

169

names of anyone who'll give them and any problems we need to pray for."

"What's in your bag?"

Brad lifted a plastic Zip-Loc up for him to see. "See, everyone gets two protein bars, a bottle of vitamins, and a ten dollar gift card for Burger King. They also get a copy of the Book of John."

"The Book of John?" Jeff chuckled. "You really think that will help them?"

"More than the other things, Jeff. Man can't live by bread alone."

The freeway bridged a dry stream bed lined with small trees and shrubs. Camping tents of many colors extended from the overpass along the side of the gulch. No one seemed to pay any attention to them. Brad pointed to the bridge. "Let's start under the cover and work our way out along this bank."

Jeff grinned at him. "You think they'll believe you're Santa Claus?"

Brad ignored the sarcasm. "You're on this team too. Write down first names and any problems and worries they might talk about." Jeff shrugged.

The first man was rocking back and forth and looking out toward the sunlit tree tops. He was portly, sported a scruffy beard, a concert t-shirt that almost covered his belly, and pajama bottoms. He was mumbling to himself.

Brad stood beside him and asked, "So, what's happening, man?"

No answer for a few moments, then without looking at his visitors the man said, "It's beautiful—they're dancing now."

"What are you on, friend?"

"California Sunshine. Crazy colors now--look."

"What?"

"You know—Pink Panthers."

Brad turned to Jeff who was laughing. "Translation?"

"Sure. He's on LSD. Can't you tell?"

"I thought they called that 'acid'?"

"Maybe if you're a Boomer."

Brad tried unsuccessfully to make eye contact with the man. "What's your name?"

"Go by Tom-tom. Got any Zen for me?"

"Don't think so--just something for your health. We'll check in with you next time." He put the water and the gift bag beside him. "I pray God will have mercy on you."

Tom-tom kept rocking but now he sang, "Yeah, mercy, mercy--mercy me."

Brad scowled at Jeff. "Think we'll move on." Jeff laughed.

The next one down the line was an older man with a foot long gray beard that hung over a tattered camouflage uniform. He sat on a folding chair and squinted at the pair with suspicion. "You guys police, or what?"

Brad gave him his best smile. "No, I'm a doctor's assistant. We're here to help with your health—physical and spiritual."

"So, you're pushing Mary Janes? Don't bother me with kid stuff." He rolled up his sleeve and displayed rows of needle marks. "Unless you got Witches Teeth or Tragic Magic, get lost."

Brad rolled his eyes toward Jeff who said, "Crystal Meth or Heroine."

He made eye contact with the man. "We're here to help you get off the witchy brew stuff. My name's Brad, and this is Jeff. What do you go by?"

"I go by one high to the next. Name's Jim. Who are you with, then? The Health Department?"

"Nope, we're on our own, Jim, but if you have a health problem, or any interest in kicking the habit, maybe we can help."

"So, you're out looking to fill your rehab beds, huh? Not interested."

Brad squatted down on his haunches and made eye contact. "Jim, do you believe in God?"

"Aaah," Jim bellowed. He waved his arms gesturing for them to leave. "Now I get it. Jesus freaks! Get outa here."

None of the other homeless had settled close to Jim. About twenty feet away they found a middle aged man in jeans and a flannel shirt cooking some meat on a tiny barbeque. He smiled as they approached and said, "I could have warned you not to go near Jim. You're lucky he isn't in one of his violent moods."

Brad returned the smile. "Hi. I'm Brad and this is Jeff. We're just hoping to make a difference in some lives out here. Anything we can do for you?"

"I'm Sam." His smile turned into a thin lipped grimace. "Sure. You could give me my ninety thousand a year management job back, and my house—and while you're at it, I'd like my wife back, too. Lucky I don't have any kids."

"Good, Lord, what happened, Sam?"

"My company reorganized and I got laid off. I thought I could make it up with a get rich quick scheme. Don't tell me—I should have known. My signature covered the debts of the whole thing."

"So, you lost everything?"

"No, before the truck pulled up at the house I threw all the personal stuff I could find in the back seat of my car. While they loaded up I grabbed my camping equipment –and my dog." He gestured to a black Lab sleeping behind him. "Sergeant's the only one who loves me now."

"That's not true. Jesus loves you."

"And where is He?"

Brad held out one of his bags. "Jesus sent you some water and granola bars for starters, but more important, here's His word, too. Be sure to thank Him."

"Yeah, well thanks. You're nice guys. This will supplement my lunch here."

Jeff peered at his grill. "What's cooking?"

"I picked out some hamburger and chicken pieces from the dumpster behind a restaurant. In the interest of health, I give them a good grilling first."

Jeff chuckled. "That's all you eat every day?"

"Oh, no. Most days I get enough panhandling or selling some of my belongings to hit a fast food place and get a bag of dog food for Sergeant."

"Too bad he doesn't earn his keep."

"Oh, but he does. His begging eyes bring in the sympathy cash, and he helps keep me warm at night."

"Did you sell your car?"

"No such luck. Impounded by the court—and I thought I had it well hidden, too."

Brad made eye contact and lowered his voice. "Look, Sam, we want to help you get on your feet. Have you tried to get a job?"

"I'm on the wait list for a County maintenance job."

"Good." Brad grinned. "Can we pray for you?"

"Sure, put me on the list."

Brad moved closer, put his hand on one shoulder and motioned for Jeff to do the same. Sam was startled. "You mean right *now?*"

"Right now, brother."

THIRTY NINE

A lone teenager sat by herself in a large room where many women would arrive a few hours later. Katie was playing video games on the cell phone she'd been given and sat cross-legged on one of the many beds. She pretended not to notice when Martha ambled over and sat beside her. "Hi, Katie, I guess its boring being all by yourself before the ladies get here, huh?"

Martha waited patiently for a response. Katie rolled her eyes upward. "I'm okay. Used to it, I guess."

"How was your first day at school yesterday? Gina said you didn't want to talk about it when she picked you up."

"Fine."

"Did you meet anyone you thought might be a friend?"

"Not really." Katie put her phone down and looked at Martha. "Was that all you wanted to talk about?"

"No. We're just concerned about you. You must miss Jackie now that she's back in college, huh?"

A hint of a smile crossed her lips and she nodded. Martha grinned. "I thought so. We miss her, too. Jackie comes with her own rays of sunshine."

"Yeah, and she taught your art class, right?"

"She did, but Carla's going to give it a try tonight. I hear you're quite an artist yourself. Perhaps you could help her out?"

Katie's face brightened. "Really? You'll open up the art room?"

"Yes, and I talked with Pastor and we'll leave it open for you all day so you can paint anytime you want."

"Hey, that's so cool. Thanks, Martha." Katie swung her legs off the bed and rewarded her with a quick hug. "I've got a few painting ideas spinning around up here." She tapped her temple. "So, is it okay if I use your drawing paper and an easel?"

"Of course. Look, we know this place isn't a real home, but hopefully, you'll only have to put up with us for a short while. The County told me yesterday that your foster care paperwork is progressing. Thanks to our lawyers, they have ruled your previous home unfit and are looking at suitable foster parents. Unfortunately, they still feel you should stay in Santa Barbara where you have a mother and your familiar school."

"What if this foster place is a bummer?"

Martha chuckled. "There's a two week trial period for both you and the family. They've agreed to let Christian agencies be included in your placement and I've made some suggestions for them, but that would be here in LA. Truth is, most families want younger kids, but, don't worry, we'll still find you a good home."

Katie giggled.

"What?"

"Free to good home--reminds me of an ad by an animal shelter. I'm waiting for someone to take me in, like a troublesome mutt."

Martha laughed and gave Katie's knee a little swat. "Well, what *they* don't know is that the family you get will be even more blessed than you will." She stood up. "Anything I can do for you right now?"

"Yeah, I know you said I couldn't leave the building, but isn't there some outside place I can go for some fresh air?"

"We're just worried you might wander off again and we're responsible." She pointed. "That door leads out to our garden. Promise me you won't hop the fence and you're welcome to go there any time. I'll unlock the door."

"Cool. I'm not gonna run away, Martha."

*   *   *

The garden was empty save for one young woman nursing her baby under the palm tree. Katie saw a low beach chair someone had left in the middle of the lawn and carried it to the far corner. She settled down, took out her phone and punched in a number from memory.

"Hi, Meg. It's Kat."

KATIE!! OMG, we all thought you were dead and buried in your back yard.

Katie chuckled. "Not quite. I made it out just before that happened. I'm fine, Meg. I escaped to Los Angeles--found some nice people. I'm getting by."

Oh, man, I'm so glad. You ever coming back?

"Not soon. I wish I could see my mom, though. What do you see going on across the street?"

Mrs. Sanderson? I haven't seen her for weeks. A while back she called her friend, Mrs. Kelly—told her she was sick, and she couldn't answer the front door. But, gee, I'm glad you're okay at least.

"I was hoping you could find out what's happening there, Meg. Mom doesn't answer her phone now. I was thinking, when you know Rolf is out, maybe you could go over with your laptop and we could Skype."

Sorry, I can't go over there. I'd even be scared to do that if I had a swat team. My mom says she can see evil spirits flying around the place.

"Copy that. Well, just keep an eye on the house, then. Let me know if you see anything unusual, okay?"

Sure. There are some cars that come and go—big sedans. Two or three men go into your place most every day.

"So, now I'm worried more than ever. Look, see if you can take down a license plate."

I can do better'n that. I've got a telephoto lens. "Spy Hazel" on duty here—photos to follow. Anything else?

"Yeah. My locker at school—combination is A-D-Y. Hold my stuff at your place for me, okay?"

"Roger that, Kat."

FORTY

Sam stepped up to the bank teller, cash in hand. "Hi, Ellie. I've got a little deposit today."

"Well, if it isn't Sam Copeland. I haven't seen you in awhile. I'm so sorry about what happened to you—just wanted to let you know."

"Thanks, Ellie. I appreciate that, but I quit feeling sorry for myself last night—gonna turn things around."

"I hope so, Sam. Your balance used to be in the hundred thousand range."

"True.' He chuckled. "Now I'm in the hundred dollar range, but I've come to realize that cash isn't what makes you happy. There's much better things in life. Here." He handed her two twenties and a five dollar bill. "I'm depositing forty dollars and fifty cents of this. Give me the change, please."

"Sure. Look, it's none of my business, but I'm curious. Did you get a job?"

"No. This is just from selling my golf irons, but I am working on that job idea."

"I'll bet you get one, too." She handed him the receipt with the change and studied his face with lowered brows. "Your whole attitude seems upbeat today. You meet a nice lady?"

"No, it's not about a woman." Sam grinned and turned to go. "God is real, my friend. May He bless you and your family, Ellie."

Ellie motioned for the next in line to come to the window. Her brow furrowed and she whispered to herself, "God bless you?"

Sam walked across the street and down to the corner where a Catholic church had its doors open. He entered the foyer, raised his hands overhead and said a prayer. He dropped four dollars and fifty cents into the Poor Box and laughed.

FORTY ONE

"So, are you getting married or what?"

Jackie turned around from her dorm desk, laughing. "You sure have a way of getting right to the point, don't you, Gabby?"

Gabriele finger-pointed. "You can't fool me. You're even more than your usual happy self since you came back. I see you dancing around and humming with your feet floating inches above the ground. Only one thing causes that--you're in love, girl."

Jackie's face erupted with such a smile crescendo, one could hear violin music from above. Gabby staggered back, hand-on-forehead, laughing. "OMG, that smile of yours should be licensed as a weapon."

"I just got another sweet letter from Brad. So old fashioned—it reads like one my parents used to write each other. Don't take it personally, but we have to be in a private place for those."

"I'll *bet*." Gabby gritted her teeth. "But, spill it. Will he propose, or are you gonna move in together?"

"The Lord doesn't want us fooling around before marriage. A good Christian girl like yourself should know that. Anyway, I'm sure he'll ask me but it'll be in person." She finger pointed. "Your turn, Gabby. What's happening with you and Stan?"

"Still just dating, but we don't see anyone else. His older brother has been living with his girlfriend for years now." Gabriele pulled over a chair and sat next to her. "If he asks me to live with him, I'm afraid I'd lose him if I said no."

Jackie put a hand on her arm. "Gabby, it's about *how* you'd say no. Tell him about how you feel about the sacredness of marriage. You said he's a Christian, right?"

"Yeah, and we go to church together sometimes."

"Good." She shrugged. "If he loves you, your commitments will grow stronger."

Gabriele dropped her head. "But maybe he's not sure yet. We could break up."

"Gabby." She let go of her arm and gave it a tap. "Now you're sounding like I used to be."

Gabriele looked up and smiled weakly. "I know you're right." She raised a finger and tightened her lips. "I'm a writer. I'll work on a good answer for him if he asks—something like how waiting will make our love grow stronger."

"Atta girl. Now, if you'll excuse me I've got to study for this Chemistry test. I don't know why I even signed up for this one."

Gabrielle tilted her head and produced a bright-eyed grin. "Cause your looking for that perfect chemistry?"

FORTY TWO

Brad sat in his office at Sewell's Medical Group writing a progress note. "Stopped her meds with a one ninety five blood pressure," he mumbled out loud. "She said, 'I'm feeling just fine, Doc.' This time I sure hope I made her understand how dangerous her pressure is."

The receptionist stood in his doorway and rapped on the door frame. "Uh, Mister McKinley, there's a man on the phone asking to see you."

He gave her a quick glance. "Too urgent for an appointment?"

"He's not a patient. Gave his name as Sam Copeland—said you met him in the field, whatever that means."

Recognition came over Brad's face and he turned to face her. "Oh yes, I know who he is. Did he say what was on his mind?"

"Just that he wanted to drop by to thank you and buy you dinner in exchange for more advice."

"Really? How many more patients do I have, Liz?"

"One suture removal with possible infection and a pre-op."

"Fine. Tell him to be here about five thirty."

Sam sat in the waiting room with a duffle bag beside him and a wide grin. He put out his hand to shake Brad's. "I've got some good news Doc. Can I tell you my story over dinner?"

Brad grinned back. "Sam, I'm not sure I'm ready to eat what you were munching on when we met."

He laughed. "No more stuff like that. Name a restaurant."

"Brown Cow steakhouse, not far from here. You're buying?"

"Yup. Can I stash this bag in your trunk?"

Once settled into a restaurant booth with orders placed, Brad asked, "Anyone can see you're a changed man, Sam. That's great. What's happened?"

"Well, Brad, I always was a Christian, but after reading the Book of John you gave me, this feeling of confidence came over me. I said out loud, 'If that's you, Jesus, I'll walk with you always.' I had sold some stuff for forty five bucks the day before, but that wasn't the source of my confidence. The next morning I walked over to a nearby church I'd seen—Living Water, I think it's called. I asked the pastor what I should read next."

"I think they're Pentecostal. What did he say?"

"He said, read Romans, and gave me a Bible. I was gonna just thank him and leave, but he insisted on saying a prayer for me. I promised I'd come back on Sunday."

Brad gave him a thumbs-up. "You're making my day." The waitress served them their ice teas. Brad said grace, clinked their glasses and said, "To Jesus."

"I haven't gotten to the best part. That afternoon I went to the bank to deposit my earnings but I had this strong urge to give four fifty to the church—you know, tithing ten percent--and I did."

"I like that 'best part' of your story."

"That's not it. The *next* morning I went back to the bank to take out a few bucks for lunch and my receipt showed a deposit that day for one thousand, seven hundred and fifty dollars."

"Whoa! From where?"

"It was from my old apartment manager, a damage deposit I had assumed was forfeited in my bankruptcy almost a year ago." He chuckled. "God is working in my life, Brad."

"Yahoo!" The waitress gave him a puzzled look as she put down their plates. "What are your plans for this cash, Sam?"

Sam glanced heavenward and grinned. "I used to write five hundred dollar checks to charities in the past. I'd boast about them and enjoy the tax deduction, but I've never felt so good as when I put a hundred and seventy five dollars in an unmarked envelope in that plate at Living Water last Sunday."

"I think God said this about tithing: 'Test me in this.' Sam, your story is making *my* faith stronger. What's next for you?"

"I used to be operations manager for Digby Construction and I was good at it. My plan is to get a cell phone and apply for jobs like that, but I need an address and access to a computer. Got any advice for me?"

"There's a men's mission on Fourteenth and Olive and they'll allow you to have a dog. Start staying overnight there and you can use their address for your own. They don't have any advanced services but I think I can get you access to a computer if you don't mind going to a ladies mission."

Sam grinned. "Super. Let's go. Would you mind helping me pick up Sergeant and my belongings from the 'lost gulch' and dropping me off at that men's mission?"

"My pleasure, and I can't wait to tell Jackie about this."

FORTY THREE

Just before noon the next day, Brad and Sam were being waved in at Martha's door. Brad put his hand on Sam's shoulder. "Hi, Martha, this is Sam Copeland, the man I talked to you about on the phone."

She stood up behind her desk and reached over to shake Sam's hand. "Welcome, Sam. We're all about getting the homeless back on their feet." She grinned. "Men's feet, too."

Sam returned the smile. "Thanks. I sure appreciate your help. I could use an hour a day of computer time, but I'll take whatever you say."

"We don't have a time schedule but just call first." She pointed to a woman whose back was turned towards them. The woman was busy tapping on a computer and muttering to herself. Martha said, "Right now as you can see, it's in use, but I think she'll be through in a few minutes." Martha gestured for Sam to sit on a side chair.

Brad gave Sam a thumbs-up. "Okay, I think my job's done here. You know the bus route back to the mission and you can call me anytime."

Sam returned the upturned thumb. "Can't thank you enough, man."

"Absolutely my pleasure. God be with you, Sam." He gave a wave before heading out the door. "And thanks to you too, Martha."

. After about ten minutes, the woman swiveled around to face Martha. It was Gina. She said, "Sorry I took so long. I was researching places I might live. Did you ever hear of a place in Georgia called Opportunity Town?"

Martha put her hand under her chin. "I think I read an article about them last year."

"They have an interesting plan for rehabilitating the homeless. Those who are off drugs and are able to work can rent these tiny cute two room houses."

"They can pay rent?"

"Yes, the mission has several retail stores and such and they get paid to work in them for what they call OT dollars."

Martha chuckled. "So, no buying drugs down at the corner."

"Right, but they earn savings as well so later they can move out into the world."

"You're not thinking of moving to Georgia, are you?"

"Nah." She shook her head. "I wouldn't want to move to far from my new friends, but after a few paychecks…" She looked up at the ceiling. "Thank you Lord. I'll rent a room from a single woman. I found a few possibilities."

Martha grinned and wiggled her hands beside her face. "I can't tell you how happy it makes me to hear that. You start your position next week, right?"

"Sure do." She hit the print key. There, that's the lesson plan for the assistant principal. I should be all ready for Monday."

"Nervous?"

"Well…" She dropped her head. "I didn't think I would be, but yes."

"Ah, you'll be fine." She gestured toward Sam. "Oops. How rude of me. I should introduce you two since you'll be sharing time on our computer. Gina, this is Sam Copeland. He's looking for a job like you were."

Gina was startled, not realizing he had been behind her all along. Wide-eyed, she extended her hand to him. "Oh Hi, I'm Gina Giannopoulos. I'll only be here in the evenings next week since I'm starting work."

Sam kept the eye contact going. "That's so great, but now I'm jealous. I hope to be interviewing for positions in corporate operations. Where will you be working?"

"I'll be teaching at Sunrise Middle School. It's a Christian school that believes in second chances, and I'm not going to let them down." She tightened her lips and raised a fist. "I'm impressed with your ambitions, Sam. Corporate operations? You must've done that before."

"I have, but corporations are less likely to take risks on applicants who aren't currently working. However, I'm planning to impress these guys, and I've found a God who gives second chances."

Martha watched this exchange tilting her head from side to side as each one spoke. "All right, Gina, better let him get to work."

Gina didn't look away from Sam. "Martha used to be a school principal. Can you tell?" She giggled. "Look, I'm about to scoot down to Del Taco and pick up something for lunch. Can I get anything for you?"

"Hey, great. I'll take a Beef Macho Burrito and a Coke."

Gina gave Martha a quick glance and a finger point. "Fish Tacos, right?"

"Uh huh--sure."

Sam handed her a fifty dollar bill. "But, I'm buying. It's the least I can do for you nice ladies."

Gina put the money in her purse and returned a silly grin with a curtsy. "Why, thank you, kind Sir."

When she left, Sam sat at the computer but turned toward Martha. "She sure is a sweet woman, huh?"

Martha shrugged with a pout, but she batted her eyelashes.

FOURTY FOUR

Pastor Duncan McKinley, Brad's father, concluded the sermon he called "God's Timing," and gave the congregation a parting prayer. Brad joined others chatting in the aisle and working their way toward the exit.

A man standing along the back wall gave him a wave and Brad headed for him. "Willie!" Fist bump. "How's the 'miracle man', huh?"

"Riding on His grace, man—just riding' on."

"That's so great. I want to hear all about what's been happening, but first I want you to meet my dad, the pastor."

They moved to the church foyer and waited for others to finish talking with pastor at the door. Brad said, "He'll be with us in a minute, but tell me how you knew this was my church."

Willie pulled out a card and held it up. Brad chuckled. "Oh, yeah, my scripture cards. I gave you one, didn't I? What's that one say?"

"It said that nothing can separate you from the love of the Lord."

"So true—oh, here's Dad." He held Willie and his father by their shoulders. "Dad, this is William Clark. He's the miracle healing I told you about."

Pastor Duncan took Willie's hands in his. "Welcome, Willie. Our congregation would love to hear your story first hand one day. Are you just visiting with us today?"

"Yeah, I'm going to a Pentecostal church in Azusa where I live now. I've been meaning to look up Doctor Brad. I owed him a thank you and an update."

"So glad you came, Willie." He released his hands with a squeeze. "Brad's told your story to anyone who'd listen. I'd guess you're still walking with the Lord."

"Well, Pastor, I suppose some might walk away if they just heard about Him, but it sure is different when you meet Jesus in person." He grinned.

Duncan chuckled and motioned toward some sofa chairs in the lobby. "Now *I'm* jealous. Sit awhile and bring us up to date."

Willie sat with a sigh. "Well, I think you know that Doc Brad put me up at his place for a few days then got me signed in at Mission Dignity on Fourteenth Street. They loved hearing my witness in their chapel and I joined their prayer team."

Duncan said, "You said you moved to Azusa, though."

"Right. Social Services at the hospital couldn't find any of my relatives, but *Sally* did. She's an ER receptionist"

"Oh, yeah, I know her," Brad said. "She makes things happen when she's on duty—treats the patients like family."

"Yeah, well, Sally did some ancestry searching for me and found a second cousin living in Azusa. She went right ahead and called them, too. They came and visited me at the Mission and told me they wanted me to stay in their guest house."

Pastor Duncan was smiling. "Oh, I feel the Master's hand at work here."

"Maybe. Anyway, I was reluctant but they said I was an answer to *their* prayer for someone reliable to help at their house."

Duncan gave a knowing smile and a nod to his son.

Willie continued. "My cousins, Jon and Sonja Wright, are missionaries to the Indian Reservations, and their son had been in charge of their house when they were away. He got married and left for Texas, so they would have to leave their house empty when they were gone."

Bras said, "Great. So, now you're in charge?"

"Right. I take care of security and their landscape when they're home. They also let me take care of Boomer, their Golden Retriever, but he thinks he owns me."

Duncan and Brad laughed. Duncan asked, "So you have a full time job, huh?"

"Part time. I have another part time job with an irrigation company and I'm working on getting back into computer repair." He stood up. "I'll come back and visit another time, but I have to get going."

Brad gave him a quick hug. "Now I see what Jesus meant when He said you'd be starting a new life. Do you have to work this afternoon?"

"No, but Boomer said I could only be gone four hours."

FOURTY FIVE

That same Sunday morning Jim and Nancy Rogers were walking out of *their* church with Katie beside them. "Now, Katie," Nancy turned to their guest. "I hope you don't think we have you over every Sunday just to get you to go to church."

Katie raised a finger and met her gaze with a smile. "Oh, but I do, Mrs. Rogers, I do, but I don't mind."

"Well, good, because the truth is we really enjoy your company, and I love to watch you paint in our back yard. Did you hear God's message of love for all today?"

"Oh, sure. I also heard 'ya better obey or fry,' right?"

Jim laughed and Nancy bit her lip. He opened the car door for his wife. "Can't argue with that, Katie, but following Jesus gives you an inner peace—while it also keeps you out of the fry pan."

Katie bounced into the back seat of their Mercedes. "Well, the band makes me feel good, especially that white-haired guitar player. He tosses in great improve riffs in their songs. But, next week, can I go with the others my age before the sermon?"

Nancy leaned over in her seat to face her. "Yes, I was going to suggest that very thing. They have a great youth pastor, but I didn't want you to think we were passing you off. Is there anything else that bothered you beside the long sermon?"

"Yeah, that boy in the row ahead of ours. He kept turning around and leering at me."

Jim said, "That's the down side of being beautiful, Katie, but I can speak to his dad. Meanwhile, try to develop a thick skin."

Katie laughed and Nancy squinted at her. "What?"

"I just pictured myself growing real elephant skin. No boys would bother me *then*, would they?" They all laughed.

When they got home Katie said, "You know, Mrs. Rogers, you don't have to make a fancy meal every Sunday. I'd be fine if we just had sandwiches or lunch at a restaurant."

"Nonsense. You should know how much I love to cook, especially when it's for more than us two. You give me an excuse and I enjoy it."

"Good, 'cause I'm getting used to it."

"Actually, I'm feeling guilty myself," Nancy said. "I hope you didn't think you had to pay us back by starting on that portrait for us."

"You kidding?" Katie chuckled. "I live for my art, and I've never painted on real stretched canvas before. That musta cost you a couple hundred bucks, huh?"

Jim lifted his hands. "It did, but I thought that's what everyone used."

"Nah, we mostly use Gesso boards but you can't beat the real quality of framed canvas."

"Well, see, we're just being selfish cause the portrait is ours and we want it to last. But, say, how long do you think it will take you?"

"I'm supposed to be back at the mission by five, so with only a couple of hours to work each week, I'd say maybe two months."

Nancy turned to her husband. "Jim, why couldn't we have Katie visit us on Saturday, too? She could stay overnight and have more time to work."

"Fine by me." He gave Katie a questioning look. "But would you want to, Katie?"

She studied the ceiling and pouted. "Oh, I don't know."

Nancy rested a hand on her shoulder. "Please say yes. We'd love to spend more time with you."

Katie covered her delight with a prissy look. "Um, well, *maybe* if I can watch movies in your home theater and use the hot tub."

More laughing.

FORTY SIX

Sam looked up from the computer in Martha's office with a huge smile. "Wow, they want me for a second interview at Botero Plastics, Martha. I'm trying not to get my hopes up, but working with them would be just what I do best."

"Well, you know with all the prayer support you get here, we'll take all the credit."

"Ha, ha. Take all the credit you want. They gave me a new number to call to set up the appointment and I'm supposed to Email back a confirmation. Would it bother you if I made the call right here?"

"Not at all. I'm as anxious to get the news as you are."

"Thanks." He walked toward the doorway. "I'll just step out in the hall."

Sam punched in the number on his cell phone. "Operator, this is Samuel Copeland. I'm to make an interview appointment. Can you connect me with Darrel Wilkins?"

It will be just a moment, sir. He's on another line. Will you wait?

"Of course."

Just then, Gina came walking down the hall. As she headed into Martha's office she gave him an overly enthusiastic wave and a big smile. He kept the phone on his ear but returned the smile and nodded back.

Martha was working on some paperwork but looked up when Gina came in. "Hi, I didn't expect to see a busy teacher during the week."

"It's four o'clock, and I got off early. I left a bunch of photos in the picture file, Martha. Would this a good time to put them in a zip drive?"

"Sure." Martha crooked her finger to draw Gina close, and whispered, "Sam just has to do one more thing on the computer when he's off the phone. He might be getting that corporate position. I'm afraid you'll just have to wait and talk to him."

"I see." Gina snickered. "You're enjoying this, aren't you? Think I should sit on your desk and kick my legs out?"

Out in the hall, Sam said, "Hello, Mister Wilkins, Sam Copeland here. Thank you for giving me a second interview, Sir."

Sam, we were all impressed with your interview and qualifications. This second interview is with Vice President, Donaldson. Should be just a formality. You have the position if you want it.

"Oh, absolutely. I accept. Thank you Mister Wilkins. I won't disappoint you."

I know you won't. Come by tomorrow at ten. We'll give you an orientation after you talk with Donaldson. I'm sending you an Email for you to confirm.

"I'll be there, and thanks again."

The ladies gathered what was happening and stood waiting for him when he came back in. Sam raised a fist above his head and said in a hoarse voice. "I am now the assistant manager of Botero Plastics!"

He began to dance in place and the women joined in. Gina gave him a hug with her congratulations and he returned a kiss on her cheek. She said, "This calls for a celebration, right Martha? It's our turn to take Sam out for dinner."

"No question," Martha beamed, "but you two go on. I have to be somewhere else tonight."

Gina and Sam knew perfectly well what Martha was doing and gave her a look that told her so. Sam smiled at Gina. "It's early for dinner. When we finish our computer work, how about we go for a walk in Freedom Park to work up an appetite?"

Their eyes locked. "Lead on, Mister Manager."

FORTY SEVEN

"Tilt!" Carla hollered.

"No, I win." Katie leaned on the ancient pin ball machine and beamed up at her adversary." "What's 'tilt', anyway?"

Carla replied, hands on hips. "It's when you bang on the machine to make the ball drop. Quit doing that and lets go three out of five."

"Ahh, sore loser. Who told you that, anyway?"

"The *rule* book. I used to play these all the time when I was a kid. If this machine had working lights the tilt sign would be flashing and your ball would be cancelled."

Katie chuckled. "Okay, I'll give you two more games, but let's take a break. You still gotta share that box of Goobers with me."

Carla put her arm around Katie's shoulders as they left the activity room. "You drive a hard bargain, little one, but you should save the sweets for after dinner."

"You're sounding like my mom, but I bet you'd like to dive into the box yourself."

Back in the bunk room, Carla sat beside her backpack on her cot, and pulled out the box of Goobers. "I'm saving my half for the movie they're showing after chapel tonight. Too many of these will give you pimples, you know."

"Nice try, but I want to keep boys away anyway." Katie held out cupped hands. "Divvy up."

Carla poured out half her box of chocolate covered peanuts. "There, promise kept, sweetie."

Katie laughed and popped one in her mouth. "Mmmm."

A woman from the church staff walked up to them. "Miss. Sanderson, Martha wants to speak to you in her office. She said it was important."

"Miss. Sanderson? When did I stop being Katie? Is this about getting a foster home?"

"She didn't say—just that it's important."

Katie hopped off the cot and faced Carla. "I'm hoping they do like I asked and give me one near here."

"I hope so too, dear. We'll all miss you if you move back north."

Martha Eldridge got up from her desk when Katie arrived. Katie bounced over to her. "I hope its good news about a home near here." She noticed Martha's uncharacteristic stone face. "Uh, oh. Did I do something bad?"

Martha ushered her down the hall. "You did nothing wrong, Katie. I just have something to tell you in private." She opened a door beside the sanctuary and gestured for Katie to go in.

Panic came over Katie's face. "This is the cry room. Oh, God, you're not sending me back to Santa Barbara, are you?"

Martha grasped her shoulders and looked into her eyes. "Katie, Social Services called me an hour ago—but it happened the day before yesterday. Your mother passed away. I'm so sorry, dear."

Katie crashed down on a couch, motionless, unable to talk.

Martha sat down close beside her and whispered, "I know. I know, dear."

Katie shook her head side to side and croaked, "He *killed* her. I know he did."

"Now, now—you don't know that."

Eyes blazing, she locked her gaze on Martha. "He *did!*"

Martha patted her knee. "Your brother's been called. He's coming home on emergency leave."

"Hope he brings his rifle." Katie dropped her head and remained quiet for a few moments. "What am I supposed to do now, Mrs. Eldridge?"

"The funeral is in three days at Rainbow Methodist Church. Your mom was a member there."

"I don't want to go back home. I could really lose it, big time."

"Of course not. You won't have to go alone."

Katie flung herself back on the couch and made eye contact. Her voice became muffled. "But, right now—right now I'd like to be alone for awhile."

Martha got up and gave Katie's shoulder a little squeeze. "Of course, dear. Stay as long as you like."

When she left, Katie got up and paced around the room. She blew out a deep breath and wondered to herself why wasn't she crying. She took out her cell phone and dialed her friend, Megan.

"Hey, Meg, it's Kat. Things are blowing up. What do you see across the street?"

Kat! I was gonna call you tonight. Don't know what's happening but a lot of people have been coming and going for days. I got some pics of license plates for you. Right now there's a moving van in your driveway. Maybe your mom's leaving.

"You don't know, huh. Mom died in the hospital two days ago."

OMG, Kat, that's horrid! I heard an ambulance that night but my bedroom's in the back. Oh, geese, I'm so sorry. You coming back for the funeral?

"Maybe. Not sure yet. Text me those plate shots."

FORTY EIGHT

A blue Mercedes sedan pulled into the parking lot at Saving Grace. Brad got out of the driver's seat and opened the rear door for Nancy Rogers before her husband could get there. "I'll walk you guys up to Martha's office. She'll know where Katie is."

Martha didn't, but said she promised not to wander away. They found her in the garden talking to Carla who was standing at an easel, painting. Katie embraced the Rogers in silence before Nancy whispered, "Oh, my Dear, we're so very, very sorry."

Brad said, "Don't worry about having to see Rolf, Katie. You got big muscle with you on this trip."

Katie looked at him with a thin-lipped smile. "Good. I'm going--ready whenever you are."

"And, don't worry. I'm not taking you in my clunky car. Jim's letting me drive us all in his big Merc. Besides, I heard he's got a compartment in the trunk lid full of AK- 47s."

Jim laughed.

The men rode in front, Nancy and Katie in the back. Katie said, "I haven't slept much lately. Hope you don't mind if I catch some zz on the way."

"I thought so. We came prepared." Nancy had a pillow on the seat and moved it to her lap. Katie laid her head on it, curled up like a kitten and slept all the way to Santa Barbara, helped by Nancy who hummed lullabies and massaged her shoulder.

Jim had three rooms reserved at the local Hilton for them. While they had lunch nearby, both Jackie, and Katie's brother, John, showed up within minutes of each other and joined them.

After a quick kiss, Jackie and Brad sat together at the table whispering conversations not meant for others.

When John came in wearing full marine fatigues, Katie jumped up and gave him a hug. "Sis, I'm so sorry I couldn't be around home when all this was going down. Maybe I could have done something."

"Me too, but don't blame yourself. I'm the one who ran away."

"This isn't our guilt trip Kat. It's all Rolfs fault. Look, I plan on spending the night at our house. I'm not the least bit afraid of that creep, but maybe one of your friends could drop me off?"

Jackie said, "I've got my little car here. We four can fit if it's all right to go with you."

Katie raised her hands. "Course it is. We could use the backup. I assume Johnny will pass out the weapons."

Jackie bared her teeth as they all stood up to leave. "Okay, then." She turned to her parents. "We'll be back and visit you at the hotel, but just so you know, Brad and I are going out tomorrow night. When is the funeral?"

Jim replied, "Day after tomorrow at ten."

*   *   *

With John giving directions, it wasn't long before they were pulling up to John and Katie's home. There were no cars in the driveway and the garage was closed.

John got out quickly and looked back at them through the window. "I've got the keys in case Rolf's not home. According to the neighbors, Rolf's probably moved out. Why don't you all come in for awhile?"

They stood on the front porch, waiting, but there was no response to the doorbell. John took his keys out and tried to open the front door. "Darn. Rolf's changed the locks."

Katie was peering in the window. "Johnny! There's no furniture in there."

"What the heck. Wait here, I've got back door keys too."

In a minute, John returned, shaking his head. "No luck—and our cat, Pookie, is on the back porch. Don't look. She's dead. I'll come back and bury her later." He held up a finger. "Just a minute, I'll go and check the windows, too."

Katie leaned her head against the front door and the long postponed tears began to come. Jackie embraced her as she sobbed. "My, God, he's taken *everything*, Jackie—(sob)—my mother--my home—even my *cat*."

208

"Jackie said, "No, not your spirit, Katie, and not your life."

The big sobs finally came. Jackie held her tight and began to cry as well. Katie rasped, "I let her down—my mom—and she was the *only*—the only person who--who loved me."

FORTY NINE

John appeared from behind the house, walking grim faced and punching on his phone. "Windows all locked. They even put a padlock on the tool shed. I'm calling our family lawyer." He held out the phone. "Here, it's on speaker."

"Hello, this is John Rogers. I need to speak with Counselor McLaughlin about an urgent matter."

A woman's voice: "Oh, Hi, Johnny, I forgot. You're all grown up, now. Terrible thing about your mother. We're all so sorry."

"Thank you Elaine. Is Counselor available to talk?"

"Oh, I think so. He's in the library—well it's really our break room, but with a few law books there, he calls it a library."

"So, can you put him on? It's really important."

"Oh, sure." She calls, "Sean? Counselor, I've got Johnny Sanderson on the line. Can you speak to him?" A Pause. "He'll be right there."

Gravely man's voice: "Johnny, so sorry for you loss. Do you know where Katie is?"

"Right here, Sir. We're on speaker."

"Oh, good. Glad you're back, Katie. Are you calling about your mother's estate?"

"Yeah, we just got here and found our house is empty and locked up."

He coughs. "Well that's strange, but I wouldn't know anything about it. See, your mom changed to another law firm two weeks ago."

"What?" Katie interjected. "She would never do that."

"Well, she did—all legal and proper. No hard feelings, by the way."

John replied, "Look, no one called me. This is starting to smell. What law firm, and who's our new family lawyer?"

"Your lawyer is Sterling Howe of Howe, Cheatham and Dewey. They're one of the largest in Los Angeles, but they have a satellite office here. It was founded by Dewey's father, but when Howe joined the firm, they had to..." He chuckled. "Reverse the order of their names."

Brad and Jackie both snort-laughed, but John continued. "Very funny, but I'm not feeling humorous, right now. Should I call them?"

"Sterling told me he'd meet you in his office after the funeral. Real sorry about your loss, Johnny—you too, Katie."

John said, "Thanks for the info. Good Bye." He looked at the others and let out a big breath.

Brad opened his hands toward John. "I've got twin beds in the room Jackie's parents got for me. You can bunk with me, but I've got something we should follow up together."

"Thanks. What's that?"

"As her son, you are entitled to look at your mother's hospital record. I'm thinking we should give it a good going through."

Katie whispered. "Oh, yeah."

FIFTY

Rainbow Methodist Church was a small wooden structure out in the country and in need of fresh white paint. Those attending Rita Sanderson's morning funeral easily fit into the front row. They included Meg and her parents and three of Rita's friends. Jackie sat next to Katie, Meg on the other side. Of course Brad was beside Jackie as well. Her hand found his and the squeeze was thanks for the strength of his presence.

The minister stood beside the box of ashes—all that remained of Katie's mother and the hope of a family. Rolf did not attend. "Dearly beloved, we are gathered today in the presence of our Lord…" His remarks were brief and there were no eulogies. He concluded at the grave site behind the church and, of course, expressed condolences to John and Katie.

From there they had a buffet lunch at Meg's house. She popped a deviled egg in her mouth and turned to her friend. "Honestly, Katie, I didn't know your mom was even sick. I saw her working in the garden only a month ago."

"That's just it, Meg. We didn't either. We're gonna check with the hospital tomorrow."

"It's just so sad. Say, any chance you could move back here?"

"Maybe—depends on where they find me a foster home."

Meg's eyes brightened. "So maybe you could live with *us*, huh?"

"Oh. Meg." She got a quick hug. "You might be the only reason I'd like to stay around here, but they told me your dad's prison time rules him out."

"Darn."

John raised a finger. "Hate to bring this up, Sis, but we've got a two o'clock appointment."

"Okay," Katie gave Meg another hug. "I'll see if I can come back tomorrow after we check with the hospital."

Attorney Howe's office occupied one of the largest, most modern buildings in Santa Barbara. John and Katie went to see the lawyer by themselves, partly to give Jackie and Brad some time alone.

Katie's hands and nose pressed against the walls of the glass elevator as she watched the interior courtyard appear to shrink below. "Gosh, I've seen this building a thousand times but I never knew this was inside it."

"Yeah, only the most well heeled can afford the rent here, and that's not us." They stepped out of the elevator into a small lounge. "Katie, we're twenty minutes early. I want to talk to you about the estate before we go in there."

John sat on one of the purple velveteen couches and Katie bounced down beside him. "Sure, Johnny, but all I know is that my share is in a trust 'til I'm eighteen."

"Right. I talked to mom before I was deployed a year ago. She said that dad had left savings of about a quarter million, but she had to dip into it and there was only a hundred ninety thousand left."

"Only? Sounds pretty good to me."

"Not only that, but mortgage on the house is almost paid off and I have a key to her safe deposit box. She said the jewelry there is for you but I get the man's watch."

"Oh goody. No trust restrictions on that, huh? Did you ever see Grandmother's ring? It's gorgeous."

"No. but I'm sure you're right. Look, I wanted you to know where we stood before meeting this new lawyer. I'm the executor, but I'll bet this fancy firm will want to take a percentage, so back me up."

The young brother and sister couldn't help but gasp on entering the attorney's reception room. French provincial furniture invited the weary, and the work of master painters hung on the walls—the originals. Katie oohed and aahed as she studied the works of art while John registered their arrival with the secretary.

As soon as they sat on the Louis the Fourteenth divan, a girl appeared from a side door with coffee and a tray of nibbles.

215

"Welcome, Sanderson family." She smiled at John. "If you're over eighteen, I can offer you some beer or wine."

"No, that's fine. I'm good."

Katie said, "Do you have a Coke?"

"Why of *course* we do." She seemed so excited. "I'll be right back, Darling."

John looked at his sister with lowered eyebrows. "Is this place making you uneasy or is it just me?"

The girl bounced back in with Katie's Coke. "Now if there's anything else you need just wave at the secretary. They should call you in five."

Katie took a sip of her drink. "I think they're just super nice."

"Yeah, well, the last time the hairs on the back of my neck tingled, the enemy was crouching behind a bush ready to ambush my Company."

The secretary came around her counter, faced them and spoke with honey tinged words. "Attorney Howe is ready to see the Sanderson's now. Please follow me."

The counselor met them at his door. He was portly, but his grey pin-striped suit was tailor made to fit perfectly. His black hair was slicked back like a character from Grease. "Ah, yes, Katrina and John Sanderson," he said with a pained smile. "Please be seated."

Howe sat behind his desk and leaned forward, his hands clasped in front of him. "I hated to impose on you on the day of the funeral, but we are on a schedule."

"That's all right." John pulled out some papers from a file folder he'd brought with him. "As executor, I brought my copy of mom's will. I understand I'll need 'Letters Testamentary' in order to distribute the assets."

Howe held out his hand as though he were blocking an unwanted sunbeam. An evil grin spread over his face. "My dear children," John's neck did a tingle dance. "That won't be necessary. You see, Mrs. Sanderson made out a new will a month ago."

John rose to his feet. Howe rose up as well and slid two documents across the table toward them. "It should not surprise you that Rita left all of her estate to her loving husband, but, of course, you are included as well."

John's eyes of steel met Howe's. "*Not* a loving husband--a cruel thief."

Katie stood up beside him, a hand over her mouth. "No, no, mother would have told us." She looked at the last page. "And that's *not* her signature."

"Three witnesses say it is. I understand you're upset, but it's customary for the surviving spouse to be the beneficiary."

John's gaze remained centered. He leaned closer and spoke louder. "And our home is gone, too, right?"

"Following her death, her husband transferred the house to a real estate consortium and it was sold, but the contents of your individual rooms are in storage lockers. The key to each is attached to your copy of the will, and you'll be glad to know the estate has paid for the first month's rent. It paid for the funeral expenses as well."

John stood with clenched fists, trying to control himself and unable to speak. Katie's voice was a squeak. "So that's it?"

"No, of course not. Your loving mother left you each a sum of money." Howe slid an envelope toward John. "There are two bank accounts each with five *thousand* dollars. Katie's is a trust account with you as trustee."

John's fist hit the desk. Howe stabbed at a button. Two uniformed men appeared in the doorway and quickly moved beside John who growled, "You'll be hearing from us."

Finally, a pleasant grin spread over Howe's face. "I expect we will, and we'll be ready."

FIFTY ONE

Sunday morning, Jackie and Brad were having breakfast with Jackie's parents. "I'm feeling a little guilty." Jackie bared her teeth. "We had such a good time last night with Gabby and Stan."

Her mother raised her eyebrows. "Guilty?"

"Yeah, I mean we had just been to the funeral that morning."

Dad said, "Ah, don't feel that way. Glad you had some fun."

Mother Nancy's eyebrows remained in an upward position. "Unless you did something you *should* feel guilty about."

"Jackie laughed. Brad placed a hand on her shoulder and leaned in towards her parents. "Relax, guys. Jackie gave me the campus tour and then the art museum. We had dinner at BJ's with Gabrielle and Stan, and then found a place with a live band and dancing."

Brad gave her a quick kiss on the side of her forehead. "I had your good Christian girl home by eleven thirty."

Nancy gave a fake prissy look with a head wiggle. "And don't think I ever thought otherwise." They laughed.

"I have to say, though," Brad looked pained. "I went right to sleep, but something's really bothering John. He kept getting up and mumbling to himself. He'll be down shortly. Maybe he'll tell us."

Jackie nodded. "Katie was acting the same way, but I just assumed she was upset at having to bury their mother. She didn't want to talk last night."

Jim raised a finger. "Ah, here they come now."

Nancy waved them over. "Good morning, you two. Here's a couple of chairs. The breakfast buffet is included, so help yourself." Katie and John returned grim-faced nods.

When they came back with their plates, Nancy ventured a cheery, "How did it go with the lawyer, Katie?"

"Terrible."

John added, "Worse than terrible. We've been robbed."

"You were mugged?"

"No, Rolf stole everything. He worked with a big law firm— got mom to sign a new will that gave him all we had. It's probably fake, but who's gonna prove it?"

Brad's eyes narrowed. "We are. After church, John and I are going to get the hospital records and maybe we can talk her doctor into ordering forensic toxicology tests for us."

Jim said, "But she was cremated. You can't do tests on remains, can you?"

"Don't need them. Hospital labs save blood samples for two weeks in case the doctor wants another test, or to repeat one if there's a question."

"What are you looking for, Brad?"

Katie's hand shot up. "I know—*poison*."

"Yes, and guess what would clinch the case? The same poison might be in your cat."

Katie returned an intense look. "Go sic 'em, Pookie."

*   *   *

When the others left on their hospital expedition Katie elected to sit on a chaise by the motel pool. Jim and Nancy understood her need for alone time and sat at a table on the other side of the pool.

A waiter came over to her and Katie waved across the pool and called, "Hey, can I order something?"

"Sure, room 302. Send him back over here to sign."

She gave the waiter a smile. "A Pepsi and a small order of nachos, please, and…"

"I heard. Your folks will cover it."

Katie didn't correct him but took out her phone and called her friend. "Meg, you won't believe this. First I thought we'd have to sell the house to pay for the funeral, then--for maybe one hour--I thought I'd be rich. Ha, ha, jokes on me. Rolf stole both the house *and* Mom's savings."

Nuh, uh! How could he do that?

221

"By making a fake will."

Shoot. What's that creep say about it?

"Rolf? He's nowhere—well he's somewhere, but he must be in hiding."

But, they can trace the money and prove the will's a fake, right?

"I dunno, Meg. The worst thing is, we think he killed Mom—Pookie too."

Oh, get out. (expletive) Call the cops—but wait, I've got three license plates.

"Hold on." Katie pulled a pen out of her purse. "Go."

After giving the numbers, Meg said, *This whole thing sucks. Look, I've got to go, but one question first. Are you coming back here or not?*

"Not a clue. It depends on a foster home. Look, no offense, but there's some real bad vibes here."

Hope you stay, but I understand. Keep me scooped, okay?

"Sure will, Meg. Bye."

Katie worked on her nachos with deliberation, deep into many thoughts when her phone rang. A woman's business-like voice: *Hello, I'm Susan Miller with the Tosca Placement Center. We work with the County. Am I speaking with Katrina Sanderson?*

"Uh, yeah."

I'm told you went to your mother's funeral so I assume you are in the Santa Barbara area now. Is that right?

"Uh huh. I'm with the Rogers from L A."

Right. Could you ask them to take you to the County offices at ten tomorrow. We've found someone willing to take you.

"What? *Willing*, huh? You give 'em a Christmas bonus or what?""

Oh. gosh, I'm sorry, Katrina. That came out all wrong. I mean there's a family anxious to foster you. The caseworker will take you there tomorrow.

"Really? I was hoping for someone in Los Angeles, but are they nice?"

Well, they're fairly young. Both work and they don't have children. Previously they fostered a young boy for us for about a year.

"Okay, I guess—don't have a lot of options right now."

Great. Bring all your things and be at our office at ten.

FIFTY TWO

Doctor Walter Scoville, Rita Sanderson's attending, ushered John and Brad into his office. "I'm happy to meet you. We couldn't find any other family at the time of your mother's admission, and her husband didn't answer his phone."

Brad said, "Was he there when the ambulance came?"

"No, the driver said a friend that let him in the house and the husband was out of town. Rita was comatose when she arrived and her breathing was labored. I put her on a ventilator. Her breath had a sweet odor and I suspected her diagnosis right away."

John asked, "What was that, Doctor?"

"I believe your mother died of ethylene glycol poisoning—that is drinking anti freeze. Alcoholics sometimes resort to it if they can't find liquor."

Brad said, "Confirmatory studies?"

Walter pointed his finger at him. "I sense you're in the medical field, right?"

Brad chuckled. "Right. I'm a PA."

"Okay, then," Walter smiled and nodded. "Rita was in total renal failure. When catheterized, we got a little urine, loaded with calcium oxalate crystals—typical of this type of poisoning. She also had pulmonary edema."

"Any specific treatment?"

"We gave her a dose of 4 MP, and started hemodialysis to try and clear her blood, but she was too far gone and expired in less than an hour."

"Does the lab have any blood saved?"

"They should. Our policy is to keep it for two weeks, but we don't do gas chromatography here. You'd need that to confirm the presence of ethylene glycol."

John said, "We'll pay for that and a full toxicology."

Walter's eyebrows waved like flags. "What would be the point of that? It was a chronic poisoning over some time. Nobody slipped her a single big dose if that's what you're implying."

John replied, "Oh yeah, we're thinking a chronic poisoning over months. Mom always shared her food with her cat, and she died too."

Walter's left eyebrow remained fully raised. "You know, you might be onto something. I just remembered that the release to the funeral home was signed by the husband who was supposedly out of town."

"So, will you order those blood studies?"

"I'll get them for you. Are you going to ask the police to investigate?"

"That's our next stop, Doctor—we're going, like right now."

FIFTY THREE

With Jim and Brad in the back seat, Nancy drove Katie to the County Office. "I wish Jackie could have been here, but she has a nine o'clock class. I know she wanted to say good bye and wish you well in your new home."

"That's okay, Mrs. Rogers. Her college is nearby so we'll hook up sometime."

"Oh, I'm sure you will. You two even sound like sisters."

Jim chuckled. "No they don't. I haven't heard any good fights yet."

Brad said, "Yeah, but I'm jealous. I wish I were nearby, too."

Nancy pulled the car into a parking lot. "Here we are—the County office building. Do you want us to come with you?"

Before Katie could answer, Nancy said, "What am I saying? Of *course* I'm going in with you." She pointed to the guys in the back. "We should only be a few minutes."

When they reached the top of the entrance steps, Katie turned back and waved at the men. Nancy said, "Are you a little nervous, dear?" Katie nodded.

"This is a big moment, so we should pray." Nancy took her hands. "Dearest Lord, we trust in you. We know you will guide and protect your precious child in all things. We pray Katie receives your comfort, your protection and wisdom especially in this moment of her life, for we know you love her as we do--in Jesus name, amen."

"Oh, thank you Mrs. Rogers." Katie gave her a hug. "I just hope these folks will be as nice as you guys."

Nancy stayed with her through the registration and paperwork. A social worker came around the counter and said, "Hello, I'm Sylvia Murdock, your case worker." She nodded at Katie. "I'll be taking you to your home now."

Sylvia gave Nancy a squinted look. "And who are you?"

"I'm Nancy Rogers from Los Angeles. Our family has been looking after Katie lately. We all pray she will finds the loving care she deserves."

"That's what the foster care system does, Ms. Rogers." She gestured for Katie to follow her. "This way girl."

Katie didn't move. She embraced Nancy, gripping her firmly and holding off her tears. Her voice was strained. "I'm gonna miss you."

"Don't worry. We'll see each other again one day and I know Jackie will visit. Phone us and let us know how you're doing, huh? God bless you Katie."

Sylvia was getting impatient. "Come on, now. Time to leave."

*   *   *

Ms Murdock escorted Katie to a car in the parking lot. "Toss your backpack in the back seat, dearie. The plastic bag is from our volunteers. There are sneakers, a sweater and a couple of children's books in there along with some other stuff."

Katie got in the front. "Thank you, Ms. Murdock, but I'm a bit past that reading level."

The woman slammed the car door and started the engine. "Well, give them away then for all I care." She flashed a quick scowl. "They were just trying to help."

"Sorry, I'm grateful—really."

Murdock turned onto a large street and flashed another scowl Katie's way. "Do you know how *hard* it is to get a girl your age placed? Most families will only take the little kids. They know a teen like you can be all kinds of trouble."

"I won't be that way."

"Better not." She pulled off into a side street and entered a housing development. Pointing: "See, this is an older community, but it's close to town and in your school district."

"Looks fine."

"Darn right it is." She pulled into the driveway of a ranch style house with an uncut lawn. "You're one lucky girl."

Katie got out, picked up her pack and the plastic bag. The garage door was open and an old gray pickup stuck halfway out. They made their way to the front door amid a chorus of swearing floating out from the garage.

Murdock rang the doorbell. "Maybe the wife is in the house."

When there was no answer, she walked over to the garage muttering a few expletives of her own, "Hello! Child Services here."

"Hold on, damn it. I'm coming."

A tall, burly man came out wiping his hands on soiled jeans. "Yeah, I was just trying to fix this pile of junk. Guess who gets the good car, huh?"

He went to the door, opened it for them and shook the hand of the woman carrying the clipboard. "You're Murdock, right?" He pointed at Katie and grinned. "And this must be our little princess."

"Uh huh."

Murdock handed him the clipboard. "Mister Smith, sign the two places marked. You keep the bottom copy. You won't get your first payment for two weeks. Where's your wife?"

"I know, I know—two weeks. Wifey comes back from work at six."

"Oh, fine. Now, there's a number on the back to call if you run into any problem. On behalf of the County, we wish you well."

"Super." He grabbed Katie and bear hugged her, lifting her off the ground. "Welcome to the house."

Terrified eyes glared over his shoulder toward Murdock. "Problem," she croaked.

The woman ignored her and went out the door calling back, "Glad this worked out, Mister Smith."

He released Katie and gave her a leery grin. "Get your things, girl. I'll show you where you'll hang out."

Katie was catching her breath and gagging from the stench of brake fluid and men's cologne. "Please don't do that again."

Smith ignored the comment and grinned. "Follow me, sweetheart."

The thought of dashing out the front door to Murdock's car flashed through her mind, but she let out a breath, picked up her belongings and did as she was told.

He walked through the kitchen and she thought he was headed out the back door when he turned and opened a narrow door on one side. "I made this bedroom for our last kid all by myself."

He flicked on a glaring overhead fluorescent and they entered a six by eight foot windowless room. Unpainted walls full of holes greeted her and an army style cot took up most of the space. He grinned again. "This used to be a pantry, but I tore out all the shelves except for one and I made a clothes hanger under it. Neat, huh?"

"So, this will be my room."

"Right. It's small, but real quiet." He pointed at the plastic bag. "Toss that on the shelf above the rack."

Katie put her backpack on the bed and squeezed past him. As she struggled to get the bag over her head, Smith grabbed her wrist to help push it upward. His other hand pushed on her derriere with a squeeze. "You sure are a purty little thing," he said.

Katie realized she was trapped in a tiny room with a large, smelly, horny man and began to panic. She tried to slip past him but he held her arm. "Hey, where you going, sweetie?"

"Bathroom. Gotta use the bathroom."

"Oh, all right. Back through the kitchen and turn right. Powder room's right there."

Katie quickly secured herself behind a locked bathroom door. He stood on the other side and called out, "Make yourself comfortable. You can lie on the couch and watch TV in the den. I'll be finished in the garage real soon and we'll have a nice chat."

Katie waited until the pounding in her throat subsided. She calmed herself with prayers and a plan. When the noises resumed in the garage, she ventured out, dashed to the little room and donned her backpack.

She left the plastic bag where it was, quietly opened the back door and walked around the side of the house opposite from the garage. As soon As Katie reached the street, she jogged briskly toward her only hope of safety.

FIFTY FOUR

Brad hurried in from the scrub room knowing the operation was already well underway. Without looking up from the patient, Doctor Sewell quipped, "Nice of you to join us, Mister McKinley." The anesthesiologist glanced up with a scowl and shook his head, but the scrub nurse sighed, "Oh, doctor, didn't you know, Brad drove all the way down from Santa Barbara this morning. He was helping a homeless teen who lost her mother."

Brad took his position opposite his mentor MD. "Sorry, Doctor Sewell, I really thought I'd be here on time." He smiled at the nurse. "Thanks for the good word, Suzette. I didn't know anyone knew." He could tell she was smiling behind her mask.

Sewell grunted and said, "Pull back on the retractor, and tell me what you see."

"This is the patient we thought had a bowel obstruction, but this section of intestine looks like early gangrene. He must have a vascular infarction."

"Very good, Brad. What are we going to do about it?"

"Tie off the arterial vessel and anastamose the ends of the healthy bowel."

Suzette bubbled, "Brad, you really should go to medical school. You're half way there already."

Sewell continued, "Okay, point to where we should divide the bowel."

He pointed. "Here--where the color looks normal?"

"No, two centimeters more on each end. It's important to have good circulation so the intestine will heal properly." He reached deeper into the wound. "How's your girl doing?"

"Girl friend or the teenager?"

Sewell chuckled. "The teeny bopper. The other is none of my business, but I'd love to hear about her too. Here, feel the blockage in this artery."

Brad complied. "Quite a nodule in there. Think it's a clot or a plaque?"

"Probably a cholesterol plaque. We'll wait for pathology. So how is she?"

"Katie's been through a lot. It might turn out her mom was murdered. She's just been placed in a foster home, and we hoping and praying it works out."

"Suzette replied, "Oh, dear. I'll pray for her too."

Sewell said, "As you can see, I'm tying off the artery. Put the padded clamps on the bowel just above where I showed you and we'll remove the bad section and begin joining the good ends together."

"I'm on it, boss. As for my girlfriend, I plan on popping the big question, but she's afraid of commitment so I'm bracing for a refusal."

The surgeons worked in silence for awhile, Suzette handing them sponges and hemostats as needed. She broke the silence, speaking just above a whisper. "If she says no, I'll marry you, Brad."

Sewell snort-laughed. "Careful, I think she's serious, Mister McKinley."

Brad glanced at Suzette and crossed his eyes. She batted her eyelashes. He chuckled.

Sewell said, "Okay, that's distracting, but pay attention. We use a special technique for an anastamosis. Suzette is handing me the GIA, the gastro-intestinal stapling device. I need you to gently pull the cut ends together and hold them in position. Meanwhile you can give me a report on the homeless men you are trying to save."

"Sure. You both know William Clark, the one who was miraculously healed. Our social services found he had a cousin in Azusa, a missionary, no less. He's now taking care of their place and has a landscaping job besides."

"He's the one who actually met the Lord. Can't forget that one, Brad."

"You know, no two homeless are alike, but most don't want to try and change. Just providing housing isn't the answer, either. They all know that rehabs have those pesky little things called rules, and no drugs. Still, the best way to change any life for the better is bringing them to Jesus."

Suzette said, "Amen."

"Yeah, and that was an easy jump for Jeff and his one kidney. He sometimes goes with me and helps while I talk to the street people—am I holding this right, Doctor?"

"Yes, but now rotate both clamps ninety degrees toward you. How about the crazy ones, Brad?"

"They might be the hardest challenge, but I came across one—a schizophrenic. He's on his meds now and his family is making sure he stays on them."

"Great. Sounds like another success to me. Give me another twenty degrees rotation. You said your girl friend helps the homeless too? What's her name?"

"Jackie. She's an artist and teaches an art class at a ladies shelter. She says being creative really helps people regain self confidence. We met at a community church program."

"There, all done. You sound perfect for each other. Sorry, Suzette."

She shrugged.

Doctor Sewell explored the interior of the abdomen. "All right, Brad, look for any bleeders before you start the closure. I'll assist while you begin closing the fascia with a running suture. Did Jackie save anyone besides Katie?"

"She told me about a woman named Gina who was really depressed. With God's help, she regained her confidence and has a teaching job. Oh, that reminds me. One man who came to accept Jesus had been a successful businessman and lost everything. He started tithing on the few dollars he made on the street, and unexpected money started to come to him. Now he's back to work as a corporate manager."

"Wow, Brad. How can people *not* believe in God? Your sutures are perfect, by the way. Go ahead and finish closing the skin with staples." He stepped back. "I have to check on a post op."

"No, problem, boss."

"Just don't let your assistant distract you with any other offers."

Despite the surgical mask, they could see Suzette sticking her tongue out at Sewell. Brad laughed.

FIFTY FIVE

Jackie came back to her dorm room after a class, but was stopped in the doorway by Gabrielle. She held a finger over her mouth and whispered, "Don't know if she's asleep, but she was crying earlier."

Jackie pointed to curled up teenage ball on her bed with a pillow over her head. She whispered back. "Who the heck is that? Did you talk to her?"

"No, that's the way I found her when I came in. She was shaking and moaning, 'oh no, oh no.' I thought you'd know who she is."

Jackie gingerly lifted one corner of the pillow to peek. "Katie!"

The girl's legs shot out straight and she looked up with wide, startled eyes. "Uh, hi, Jackie." She swung her legs around and sat up.

"Katie, I thought you were supposed to go to your foster home today."

"Yeah, well, that didn't exactly work out."

Gabrielle swung over a chair to sit closer. "I heard you crying. What happened?"

"They took me to this house where they have no kids and the wife works all day. The man must weigh three hundred pounds and he's home most of the time."

Jackie sat beside her. "Well, so—maybe he's a good guy."

"So, this stranger's idea of welcoming me was a boob crushing, pelvic smashing, feet-off-the-floor squeeze."

Gabrielle shook her head. "Maybe not such a good guy."

"Ya think? Next he took me into a closet he calls 'my room,' squeezed my butt and said 'Yer awful purty.' Get the picture?"

Jackie opened her hands. "I'd have run away, too. Sorry."

"Yeah, and I thank God I was able to scoot before things got—you know-- worse. It was like Rolf all over again, so now I'm back on the street."

"Oh, *no* you're not. You've got me, my family, and the God who never leaves you."

"You know, Jackie, I did feel there was someone beside me, keeping me calm and helping me get away."

"There, see. This is the end of your being alone, Katie."

Gabrielle responded with a raised fist. "Yeah!"

Katie ventured a weak smile. "Wish you were my big sister."

Jackie let loose one of her smiles like a concussion grenade. "Let's just pretend that *I am*, okay?"

Wincing under the power of her smile, Katie chuckled. "Okay, sister, what's our plan?"

"Well, the plan is for you to come back with me to Los Angeles when I start Christmas vacation next weekend."

"All *right!*" She raised a finger. "But, could you take me to a storage locker first? I want to get some letters that show my mom's signature."

"Sure." Jackie turned to her roommate. "Gabby, do you think Bridgette has left?"

"Bridgette?" She lifted her nose up with one finger. "Yup. I saw two butlers carry her things away this morning."

Jackie giggled and pointed up. "Daughter of the ultra rich— she had a private room upstairs, but it still wasn't good enough so she left for an apartment on the outside. They won't fill it until next semester so it's all yours until the end of the week."

"Is that legal? Won't someone complain?"

"The hall monitor owes me, big time. Consider it done."

Katie laughed. "I like having a big sister."

"My pleasure, but first, we have to celebrate God helping you escape."

Gabrielle looked up at the ceiling. "Uh, oh."

Jackie pointed a finger at each of them. "*First* the three of us are heading for Dave and Busters—dinner's on me—then we party."

Katie gave a little bounce. "Isn't that where they have lots of games?"

"And rides with virtual reality."

Gabrielle said, "They've got a band, too. Count me in."

FIFTY SIX

Martha Eldridge looked up from her work at the sound of women laughing in the hall. Her door was always open and inviting. She waited to see what homeless women would walk by in such unusually good spirits.

Katie's face appeared sideways around the door frame impersonating a familiar poltergeist. "I'm baa-aaak."

Jackie and Katie stumbled into the office, giggling. Martha waved at them. "Okay, what's going on? Katie, I got a letter last week saying you were placed in foster care in Santa Barbara."

The two stood in front of her desk. "True." Katie shook her head. "That lasted six minutes, forty five seconds."

Jackie's face squinched. "Ugg, the agency made a horrible choice—they stuck her with some horny gross man who'd be alone with her every day."

Katie opened her hands. "So, I'm a runaway again." She giggled. "But this time I ran away to Jackie's dorm room."

Martha came around her desk and embraced them. "Well, you're always welcome here, child, but did you notify the placement agency?"

Jackie said, "Did we ever. My friend Gabby is an amazing writer—she's going on to a Masters in Journalism. She wrote them a real stinger and sent copies to Katie's family lawyer, the local paper and their congressman. Gabby believes in overkill."

"Well that explains one puzzle." Martha shook her head, grinning. "Both Santa Barbara police and the LAPD are looking for you. They want to bring you in for questioning."

"Sure." Katie nodded. "But I don't think it's about that. They've been investigating my mother's death. My brother and Brad have been working on it."

"Gosh, I didn't want to believe there was foul play going on, but Katie, if you want to find a place to live near here, I almost had something worked out with a Christian service. I'll get right back on it."

"Oh, I do. Thank you Ms. Eldridge."

"My pleasure, dear. Go ahead and take any bed you want for now." She flashed Jackie a hopeful look. "Can I count on you to teach an art class soon? You have a number of fans here."

"I'll start the day after tomorrow, but before I turn this little stinker over to you, you ought to know she's got a really fun side— sometimes mischievous, but always fun."

Katie gave Martha a cross-eyed grin and Martha hugged them both again. "You know I just love you both something awful, don't you?" She pointed at Jackie. "And I bet you want to head home and start decorating for Christmas, right?"

"Yeah, but not before I call my man and make sure he hasn't run off with some cute nurse. I've heard rumors."

FIFTY SEVEN

Lance Corporal, John Sanderson walked into police headquarters accompanied by his family attorney, Sean McLaughlin. John was wearing his Marine fatigues and a fresh, short haircut. They had an appointment with a Detective Jackson, a black man with twenty years experience on the force.

Jackson got up from his desk when they arrived and shook John's hand. "Sorry for your loss, Corporal." He gestured to some chairs. "Please, have a seat."

John nodded. "This is our attorney, Sean McLaughlin. I understand you have some new information on our case."

"We do. First, your stepfather works for a Mexican Cartel and his real name is not Rolf, its Rodrigo--Rodrigo Gonzales."

Sean raised a finger. "And therefore the marriage and the will are null and void."

Jackson smiled. "Yes, I assume so. The DA was able to place a hold on the assets from your home sale just before the transfer to an off shore bank. I would think you could recover them in court."

John was surprised. "Really?"

Sean said, "We will be all over that one, John. Not to worry."

"But the inheritance?" Jackson was shaking his head. "That law firm—uh—Dewey, Cheatham—they wired the assets Rolf had in joint names to a bank in the Caymans within seconds of the Death Certificate. I don't think they're recoverable. Sorry."

"Probably right," Sean said. "Best we can do is get you a tax write off."

John let out a breath. "Fine. Look, I have orders to report to Camp Pendleton at seventeen hundred hours. Have you made any progress on the murder investigation?"

"Yes and no. The blood test you were able to recover shows that your mother died of a combination of antifreeze and arsenic poisoning—same as her cat. While there was no autopsy, the hospital records note hemorrhagic injection sites on the right arm. Likely she was given a fatal injection."

John's hands shot up. "So, just find Rolf. I'll save you the trouble of hanging him since I'll shoot him on sight."

Jackson chuckled. "Your attorney will tell you about the difficulty of proving murder by poisoning, but it's a moot point if we can't locate Gonzales. We know he left for Vancouver Canada on the day Rita died, but the Cartel provides professionally made fake IDs. We notified Interpol, but he could be anywhere."

"Gotta run, Detective." John got up. "Thanks for your work and, on second thought, I can live with you're never finding that murderer. I'm content to imagine Rodrigo facing the ultimate White Throne judgement."

FIFTY EIGHT

Jackie had just arrived back at the women's mission when her cell rang. *Hi, Jackie, it's me. I just got off my shift and I wanted to tell you how much fun I had last night. Now, get ready for Saturday 'cause we're going high class and...*

"Saturday can wait, Brad. I'm over here with Katie at Saving Grace getting ready to decorate a Christmas tree. They're a little late, huh? Any chance you could come and help us? Martha can't come and even with their stepstool I can't reach the top."

Sure. I just haf'ta shower and change. Be there in twenty minutes.

Brad made it there even earlier wearing a Hawaiian shirt and a big smile—not as big as Jackie's, but big. He greeted Jackie with a swirl around hug and kiss. "Miss me already?"

Jackie gave him a shrug and a pout. "Not a bit. We just need an extra worker."

Brad laughed. He noticed Katie standing to one side. "Hi, Katie."

She extended an arm and gave him the palm-open half circle gesture. Very cool.

Brad looked up at the fir tree in the church lobby. "That must be a ten-footer and there's hardly anything on it. Don't the homeless women help out? There's no ladder?"

"They each made an ornament in their crafts class. That's all you see on there, and I couldn't find a ladder."

Katie was sliding some cardboard boxes toward them. "Ornaments in this one. The other's labeled 'angel and garlands.'"

Jackie got up on the stepstool and then climbed on Brad's shoulders. Katie handed her the tree top angel but she still couldn't reach the top. Brad took two steps up the stool but they began to sway. Katie grabbed Brad's belt. "Whoa, you two. We should get a ladder from somewhere."

Brad said, "You're sounding like a mommy. Keep hanging on, Katie. We're going for it."

Slowly reaching out and swaying with Katie making chirping sounds, Jackie thunked the tree top angel in place and wound the end of the light cord to a branch below it. Katie handed up a few more ornaments before Brad carefully came down off the stepstool. "There, see? Nothing to it. Just like the flying Walendas."

Katie held up her cell phone. "I've got the evidence right here. If you don't take me for a frozen yogurt after this, I'm telling your parents."

Jackie stuck out her tongue in response and they all laughed. Wait, who else was laughing? They turned to see a couple walking in.

Jackie waved. "Hi, Gina."

"Hi, Sam," Brad said simultaneously. "Sounds like we each know one of you."

"And, so do we," Sam said with a gesture toward Jackie. "But, I'm pretty sure you must be the young woman Gina holds in such high esteem—Jacqueline Rogers, right? I'm Samuel Copeland."

Jackie shook his hand. "My pleasure."

Gina swept her hand around. "I should have made the introductions 'cause I know all of you. I was hoping we were too late to help with the decorations."

Jackie gave her a scrunch-face. "No such luck. We were just getting started, so pitch right in. Brad told me all about you, Sam. What a rags to riches story. Maybe you could tell your story at our church before they pass the plate."

Sam said, "Mine is more like a riches to rags to riches story, but the best part was meeting Gina."

Gina took his arm and leaned into him. "That's so sweet, dear, but I think you're overselling me."

"Not at all." He kissed her on the forehead and turned to the others. "Not only is Gina female perfection, but she knows more about science and history than I'll ever know."

Jackie flashed her special smile. "Can Brad and I split the finders' fee?"

Gina said, "Sorry, Martha already claimed that—and for you two as well. She thinks her office has Cupids lurking in the ceiling."

Brad handed Sam a pile of garland. "So maybe you guys could show us how to cooperate and swing this around."

In short order the tree was ready to greet the congregation and the women being rescued at Saving Grace. Jackie insisted that the couple join them at her home and phoned in an order for three pizzas. Of course, there had to be a quick stop along the way for that frozen yogurt.

FIFTY NINE

Brad knocked on Jackie's door Saturday, a bouquet of roses moving from one hand to the other. Her father, Jim, answered the door and grinned at the man who was mumbling to himself. "Well, good luck, son."

"Uh, oh. Do you mean good luck for a wonderful date, or good luck trying to impress her?"

"Sorry, poor choice of words." Jim looked over his shoulder to make sure Jackie hadn't come down stairs. "A whole bouquet is a bit overkill. Just give her one and I'll stash the rest in a vase."

"Thanks, Jim. I just wanted to make tonight special."

Nancy came out of the kitchen and surmised what was going on in a glance. "Why, Brad, you certainly look sharp tonight, and judging by what Jackie is wearing, I'd guess you're going to a real nice restaurant."

"Deux Cheminees, but I want it to be a surprise."

Nancy giggled, went to the foot of the stairs and called up. "Jackie, Brad's here."

Now armed with a rose behind his back and a confident stance, Brad put on a loving smile and waited. Jackie descended slowly trying to be graceful but clearly unaccustomed to her new pair of black high heels. Her parents said "Have fun, you two," and disappeared.

Jackie wore a black sequined dress that came off the shoulder on one side and a lovely wavy hairdo. Her only jewelry was a thin gold necklace that bore a delicate, gold cross. Despite one ankle that kept giving away, she moved to his side smoothly and with a deep voice said, "Hi, Brad, you sure look handsome tonight."

"Whoa, Jackie, you just went from darned cute to wow-wow beautiful." He gave her cheek a kiss and presented the rose.

"Oh, that's so sweet." She gave it a sniff and asked with wide-eyed innocence, "So, where are we going tonight, handsome?"

"A secret, but I'll tell you it's French."

She attempted a demure smile. "Ooo, la, la."

*   *   *

The valet at Deux Cheminees tried to hide his sneer when Brad pulled up in a wash of smelly, blue smoke. When accepting the keys, he dangled them by two fingers like a mouse he'd removed from a trap. "You have a reservation?"

Another valet hustled to open the passenger door. "Welcome to Deux Cheminees, Miss."

Once they were inside, cordiality reigned. The maitre d' even gave a tiny bow. "Ah, Doctor Rogers, we have a special table for you this evening. Right this way."

He seated them in front of the piano and assured them live entertainment would commence shortly. Another bow and he departed. Jackie's brow wrinkled. "*Doctor* Rogers?"

"Hey, when you want a good table." she giggled.

The waiter greeted them with menus sans prices and recommended two specials. Brad thought he better not order what he couldn't pronounce, but was relieved to see the menu had English descriptions in fine print below the French.

Jackie peeked over the menu. "What are you having, Brad?"

He pointed at an item. "I'm having this chicken with sauce thing—third one down. What do you think about splitting the artichoke appetizer?"

"Perfect. Mind if I order for us?" Perplexed, Brad shrugged.

The waiter returned and grinned widely while Jackie ordered in fluent French. He nodded. "Excellent choices. I'll send the wine sommelier directly."

As soon as he left, Brad leaned forward, his mouth agape. "My gosh, you speak *French*? You never told me."

"You never asked. I took it for three years in college and two years ago my parents took us on a family ski vacation in Quebec. The food was absolutely amazing. Chef Pierre picked his own vegetables in the garden outside our hotel. I was the official family translator."

"I heard they get annoyed when Americans try and speak French there."

"Well, the young men there were very patient with me."

"Oh, I see." He chuckled. "Depends on who you are, huh?"

"And they taught me some words I never heard in class."

"Words that," His index finger popped up. "you wouldn't translate for Mom and Pop, right?"

"True." She giggled. "But one day I'm going to France." She grinned at the ceiling and put a hand on her chest. "I dream about meeting the French artists and touring all those wonderful Art museums."

A portly, bald sommelier came up behind her and, overhearing her comment, added, "Ah yes, Mademoiselle, and tonight you can prepare for your voyage with the taste of fine French wine."

Jackie grinned up at him and gave the bottle opener dangling from his neck a little flip. "And what would you recommend, Monsieur?"

"With your order I would recommend a fine Pinot Noir. For the gentleman, a Sauvignon Blanc. May I select the vintage and label for you?"

Brad's expression took on that of a knowledgeable sage. "Yeah, lets go with that, 'Missur,' but only one glass with dinner. Keep it under twenty bucks. Okay?

"Very good, sir." Brad caught him giving a quick smile-wink at Jackie.

As the couple settled into their delicious meal, they talked about Katie, Gina and Sam and, of course, Paris. The band helped by playing romantic French music. The pianist treated them with occasional smiles and eye contact.

After the main course, Jackie said, "I'm having *such* a good time, Brad, Darling. I can't thank you enough for taking me to such a special place."

"Ah, you're welcome, but I'm hoping to make this moment even more special." Brad waited until their eyes locked. "You must know by now that I am totally in love with you, Jackie." He took out a ring box from his pocket and placed it on the table with trembling hands. "I feel—at least I hope you feel the same way about me."

Jackie was silent but looked at Brad with adoring eyes. He got up and knelt beside her. The piano music stopped and those at nearby tables stopped talking and looked on. "Jackie, I'm asking you now if you will be my forever companion—my bride." He opened the box and placed it on the table in front of her.

A woman nearby sighed. Jackie picked up the box and looked at the sparkling diamond ring. "This is beautiful, but Brad, so many couples make the mistake of getting married just because they think they love each other."

Brad's face showed the shock. He held out his hand to stop the waiting musicians on the side of the room. "Uh, yes, I…"

"If that's *all* there is, love tends to fade."

Brad clutched the edge of the table. The room seemed to turn gray.

The truly *wonderful* marriages share genuine friendship, humor, partnership, common interests and a sense of spiritual oneness in the Lord."

His chin fell but he kept his eyes on his love. "I, but I hoped—I really thought…"

Suddenly, Jackie snatched the ring from the box, plunged it onto her finger and blessed him with her devastating smile. "I thank *God* we have all that and so much more. Of *course* I'll marry you!"

Brad jumped to his feet and lifted Jackie out of her seat. He waved at the waiting musicians to start. "Yeah!" They kissed. People applauded. The piano began playing as a violin and a man rushed toward them singing, "When the moon hits your eye like a big pizza pie, that's amore." (Brad's pick for romantic music.)

Brad gave her a pout. "Honey, you really made me squirm, didn't you?"

"I'm your woman now, Brad. If I've been bad, you should punish me."

He chuckled and rubbed his nose against hers. "What punishment would you expect me to dish out, darling?"

The song ended but the violinist came near them and launched into fervent peals of better chosen romantic melodies. A mysterious expression crossed Jackie's face. She put her mouth near his ear and whispered, "Tickle me."

SIXTY

Katie and the Rogers were enjoying this weekend together. After church they headed for Applebee's and slid into a booth for lunch. Jackie had carefully planned for this moment to break her good news.

"All right, everyone, I have something important I want to tell you all." She put her elbows on the table and rested her chin on her hands to expose the ring she'd been hiding. "But, gosh, I'm so sleepy this morn…"

Katie was sitting beside her. She grabbed Jackie's hand with a squeal. "OMG, you're engaged to Brad! Wow, the diamond is *gorgeous*. This is so, so *fab*, Jackie. When's it gonna be? Can I come? Please, please."

Nancy and Jim extended their hands across the table to Jackie. Nancy bubbled, "Oh, my Dear, I'm so thrilled for you. This is a forever moment in a mother's life too. May the Lord bless you and Brad."

Jim was nodding and grinning. "I was pretty sure ole Brad was planning this last night. My congratulations, darling. Have you come up with a date yet?"

"Oh, thank you guys." Jackie gave her parents a gentle version of her beautiful smile. "We're going to wait until I finish college, so we're thinking of a date in late May or June."

Jim returned a squint. "I hope you're not planning on living together."

Jackie was smiling at Katie who had captured her ring finger and was twirling the ring around. "No, Dad, we won't do that, although I have to admit it's pretty tempting."

"Well, we're just so proud of you," mother said. "And tonight's dinner has to be a celebration. I'm hoping Brad's parents can come."

"Oh, mother, that's pretty short notice don't you think?"

"Nonsense. Can't hurt to ask. Is there anyone else you'd like to invite?"

"Hmm." Jackie rested her head on one hand. "We were with Gina and Sam yesterday. You haven't met them, but I think it would be fun to have them join us."

Katie was giving Jackie an imploring look. "Uh, if I really work hard to help you get ready, maybe I could come to the wedding, huh?"

Jackie turned toward her and grasped her shoulder. "Help? I'm counting on you. Katie, if you'll accept, I want you for my maid of honor."

Katie let out a quick shriek, covered her mouth, and embraced Jackie. "Oh, Jackie—yes, yes, yes. I'm not sure what to do, but I'll do my very best. Wait, you've got a bunch of friends. Aren't they going to be disappointed?"

"They'll have to suck it up. I want you."

Tears streamed down Katie's cheeks. "Oh, thank you, thank you. You know I just love you."

No one had noticed the young waitress standing next to their booth. "I'm guessing you want a little more time to order, but if I can come to your wedding too, I'll give you a free dessert."

SIXTY ONE

Katie and Jackie were in the kitchen Sunday afternoon helping Nancy to get ready for the engagement celebration dinner. Nancy pointed a finger at her daughter. "I know meat loaf might seem rather ordinary for a special dinner, but my careful research revealed it is one of Brad's favorites. Make a note of that."

"And how would you know that, mother?"

"Simple. I asked him. Knowing a man's favorite foods is one secret to a good marriage."

Jackie yawned. "Really? That one wasn't even on my list."

Katie tried to make eye contact with a tilted head and a look of concern. "Jackie, you look beat. Didn't get much sleep last night, huh?"

"Not really. I just kept thinking about…" Yawn. "Well, just about everything."

Nancy smiled. "Oh, dear, we better let you take a nap. Katie and I can handle this."

"I'll be okay. Maybe I need coffee."

"Nonsense, Jackie. You need some milk and a soft bed." She poured a glass and motioned "run along" with her hand. "Take my sleep sound machine and the mask from my room. See you in a couple of hours."

Nancy busied herself greasing a pan and mixing ingredients and assigned Katie to snapping the ends off the green beans. She said, "Mrs. Rogers, with just the two of us, will we have enough time to make the cake?"

"I guess not. We have rice and a big salad to mix, but that's all right. I have a ton of store bought cookies."

"Couldn't your husband help?"

"Jim?" She chuckled. "Not his forte. He's busy painting our front gate. We'll be fine."

Nancy worked on forming the meatloaf and was getting ready to add the mashed potatoes on top when she saw a tear running down Katie's cheek. She pushed the pan to one side, wiped her hands on her apron and moved beside her troubled helper. "All right, Katie, the next thing we're going to do is have a sit down in the living room."

"I'm okay. It's nothing really. You're busy."

Nancy gently took Katie's hands away from the beans. "Come. Sit."

On the couch, Katie said, "I don't want to sound ungrateful--don't think that."

"Ungrateful?" Nancy placed a hand on her shoulder. "You don't want to be a maid of honor?"

Suddenly there was a bounce of enthusiasm. "Oh, no, I *do*. It's not that at all. I'm *so* excited about Jackie's wedding, it's…"

"Yes?"

Katie sighed. "I like Jackie so much. She'll be married and gone soon and I love you guys—and Martha too, but I guess I'll have to be going back to Santa Barbara again, right?"

Nancy drew her close and the girl's head fell on her shoulder. "Oh, Katie, we want you to stay here too, we really do, but Child Services has been such a bear to work with. We have a lawyer helping Martha and we're still trying to get your case transferred here, so don't give up hope, darling."

Katie blew her nose with the tissue Nancy gave her. "I won't but that placement lady up there is really mean."

"Sounds like it, but say, I called Martha and she said she might be able to join us for desert. She said she had some news for you and wanted to see you tomorrow, anyway."

Meanwhile, out at the front gate, Jim was busy sanding away when he was surprised by the appearance of Gina and Sam. "Hey, hello, you two. I didn't expect you 'til later."

Sam said, "We thought we'd come early and see if we could help."

Gina grinned. "Sam was hoping he could help you by watching a playoff game."

Jim held up a paint brush. "Maybe we'll both luck out, Sam. With the two of us painting, we should finish this in twenty minutes."

"Great," Gina said. "I'll see you inside later."

Sam knelt down and began to help sand. "Where'd all these gouges come from?"

"Yeah," Jim chuckled. "Seems Nancy thought she was feeding a stray dog. He'd come by and bark and paw at the gate until she came out."

"Not a stray?"

"Nope. Turns out he lives down the street. The owner fixed the hole in his backyard fence. But now, of course, Nancy has to visit them once a week with dog treats in her purse."

Sam pointed to a plastic tricycle beside the walk. "You have grandkids, Jim?"

"Nah. After I quit the brokerage firm, I'm now with a company that makes toys. Those plastic wheels splintered and we got sued. We'll probably have to drop that line completely."

Sam began to vigorously stir the white paint. "I hope you weren't the one picking the plastic supplier."

Jim harrumphed. "Nope. The president's cousin did that. He didn't even get bids."

"Botero Plastics makes a product that stays flexible even after years in the sun."

"Really? You could prove it?"

"We'll prove it and give you an insurance guarantee."

Jim paused, paint brush in hand and looked at Sam with narrowed eyes. You know, if you won this bid, Botero would have to supply product for an international company. That's a big volume demand, my friend. Could your company handle that?"

"That's a promise, Jim."

"So, you don't see any problems?"

"Just one—I'll have to buy a lot of champagne for the executive party."

Nancy asked Katie to answer the doorbell and, in a moment, Gina's enthusiasm was cheering them up, not to mention her whipping into the cake making. Soon they were all telling stories and laughing. A bleary-eyed Jackie ambled in, said hello to Gina, and asked if she could help with the cake.

Her mother said, "Nonsense. This is your party. Just enjoy."

Jackie looked up at the kitchen clock and let out a squeak. "Oh no, it's five o'clock. Brad will be here in an *hour* and I look terrible."

He was not late. Promptly at six, Jackie thundered down the stairs to answer the door, completely transformed with a cocktail dress, makeup, and a hint of perfume.

Brad grinned. "Hey, babe. Miss me yet?"

After a long kiss that made Katie snicker, Jackie said, "Seems like you were gone for a *week*. You know I love you just awful, big guy." Another kiss--more snickering.

The last to arrive were Duncan and Sharon, Brad's parents. By then, the painters were back inside, all cleaned up and with the game on TV. Jim and Nancy shook hands with their guests. Jim said, "Looks like we'll be part of each other's family soon. Unfortunately I'll have to start behaving now that we'll have a pastor in our midst."

Duncan chuckled. "I'm not the one who judges, you know. Say, is the game over?

"Almost and tied. Dinner's not ready yet. Come on in."

The men headed for the family room but Duncan whispered in his son's ear. "You're not included this time. Show your woman she's the most important thing in your life."

"That's an easy one, Dad. She is."

SIXTY TWO

Dinner was filled with laughter and exchanging stories of Brad and Jackie being foolish when they were children. The seven year old Jackie had painted a large puppy dog in chalk. Unfortunately it was on a bank building. Brad went through a phase of throwing insects into spider webs to see the action. Katie admitted to climbing on a neighbor's roof one night to escape an argument her parents were having. Her dad was alive then and she just watched while he scoured the neighborhood calling her name into the dark.

The stories were followed by champagne toasts to the engaged couple after dinner. When Duncan and Sharon were leaving, Pastor Duncan brought Jackie and Brad together. He placed his hands on their heads. "Can't go without giving you a prayer, all right?"

The two nodded with enthusiasm.

"Dear Holy Spirit, come into this place. We ask for your blessing on this man and woman for their protection as they walk together and with You, Jesus. Give them your joy and may they always know Thy will, Dear Lord, for they are both doers of Your will and not just hearers. We ask for Your blessing in Jesus name."

Gina and Sam also wished blessings on them as well and hugged them goodbye on their way out. Halfway down the walk they greeted Martha Eldridge as she arrived, briefcase in hand.

Martha thanked everyone for inviting her. "Sorry, I'm so late but I had trouble downloading something I have for you. I planned on surprising you with this tomorrow." She faced Jackie and Brad who stood with their arms around each other's waist. "And I'm so thrilled for you two, I can hardly stand it. She put two fists near her face and wiggle-tristed. "Oooh."

Nancy said, "We're so glad you came. I know I promised you dessert, but all I have is a sliver of cake and, uh, champagne."

"Thanks, Nancy. Maybe later." She went to Katie and grasped her shoulders. "And how are *you* doing, my dear?"

Katie grinned. "Super. I'm gonna be a maid of honor."

"My gosh, that's wonderful. You'll be the prettiest one there—except for the bride, of course."

Jim said, "Martha, we're all dying to hear what you have to tell us."

"It's a mixed bag. Do you want me to get right to it?"

"Please do." Nancy gestured toward the living room. "Make yourself comfortable. I'll get some coffee."

265

Martha sat on the edge of the sofa and everyone circled around her. "First, the bad news." She looked at Katie. "You know a Ms. Louise Murdock in Child services?"

Katie burbled her lips. "Wish I didn't."

"I guess the feeling is mutual. She claims you are a runaway and wrote a hateful letter."

"I didn't write the letter, Ms Eldridge. Gabby did."

Jackie said, "She's my roommate and I saved a copy if you want to read it. Everything Gabby wrote is true, but her style? Gabby uses a flamethrower for a pen."

Martha thought about that for a moment and nodded her head. "Murdock got the Santa Barbara police to issue a warrant for Katie's arrest."

Everyone gasped. She continued. "Don't worry, your lawyer got a judge to rescind the warrant." She pointed to Jim. "Thank you so much for hiring that man, Jim. Thanks. He is a godsend."

"What didn't change, however, is this." Martha sighed. "Murdock's service is refusing to transfer Katie's case to Los Angeles. This makes it impossible for us to set up a foster home near here."

"Oh, crap." Katie stood up. "If they think they'll haul me back and throw me to that pervert, it'll be over my dead body."

Martha motioned for her to sit. "Easy, Dear. Don't worry, that's not going to happen."

She sat and dropped her head on her chest. Jackie plopped down beside her, and put her arm on her shoulders. "Darn *right* it won't."

Martha raised a finger and her eyes brightened. "And the reason it won't is nothing short of a miracle." She opened her hands toward Nancy and Jim. "We thought it would take six months and no guarantee it would even be possible. Instead, thanks to God and your lawyer, your plan B is all approved."

"Wow," Jim said. He and Nancy shot up, glanced over at Katie and took a few steps toward Martha. He spoke in a low voice. "This is serious. No kidding—it's official?"

Martha stood up and smiled. "The papers were E-mailed to me yesterday. They're in my briefcase and all you have to do is sign and notarize them at County tomorrow. Uh, maybe you should be the ones to tell Katie."

They turned around, both with big silly grins. Nancy said, "Guess what, Katie."

Katie had been watching, open mouthed and puzzled. "Uh, you got permission to feed me to the sharks at Sea World?"

Everyone laughed. Nancy opened up her arms. "Now, Katie, it has to be all right with you, of course, but we have permission to become your adoptive parents."

Jim nodded. "Yes, and I promise to be a real Christian father to you—nothing like the terrible ones you just had."

Nancy's expression brimmed with compassion. She took a step toward her. "Katie, we love you. Please say you will be our forever daughter."

Katie sat in stunned silence for a moment then, without speaking, she leapt to her feet, embraced them both and began to sob. Nancy began to cry as well. She kissed her on top of her head and stroked her hair.

Jackie jumped up and joined the embrace. "Don't think you're leaving me out of this. You're now my kid sister--*officially*."

Jim stepped back. "But don't think we're only doing this so you'll finish painting our portraits."

When they released each other Katie was laughing. "You know I just love you guys." She looked at Jim. "I think I didn't finish it so you'd have to keep having me come over."

Nancy produced a tissue and blotted Katie's cheeks. "Oh, my dear, never, but why is there a blank space on one side?"

"I guess I'll paint the front of your house there."

Nancy said, "Maybe you could add our children. Our son will be here for Christmas soon so you'll meet him."

Jackie pointed a finger at her. "But then you'd have to include your older and wiser sister, too."

Katie laughed. "Oh really? Okay then, I'll immortalize that dynamite smile of yours."

Nancy maintained her hold on Katie's shoulder. "And you must also paint yourself into the family portrait."

Jackie brightened. "Yeah, and I'll do that portrait if you want."

Katie looked shocked. "I—Mrs. Rogers—I couldn't. I..."

Nancy gently grasped her other shoulder as well and made eye contact. "Katie, my new name is 'Mother,' and only when you join us in our family portrait, will our joy be complete."

Pascal John Imperato began writing fiction in Junior High, became a literary editor in High School, and wrote short stories in Creative Writing classes at Johns Hopkins University. Getting a Medical Degree at Duke University, and beginning a medical practice in Pennsylvania temporarily resulted in scientific and journal writing.

After a born again revelation, he resumed writing fiction, but with a messianic twist under the pen name, "John Pascal." He has published Sci-Fi, "The Revelation Trilogy" novels: "The Bee," "Domes," and "2248." Next he authored a two book angel series: "Wingin' It," and "My Child" featuring the disabled, and unwanted pregnancy respectively. "Prisoner 1171" followed, a novel focusing on evangelism in prison. Then he wrote a novella, "Fatherless," dealing with street gangs and human trafficking. The most recent story before "Adrift" was "Truth Wars," meeting the challenge of disinformation, censorship and propaganda that is trying to replace truth in our schools. All are Christian friendly.

These books are available on Amazon and Kindle. Further details at "JOHNPASCAL.com".

Made in the USA
Columbia, SC
26 May 2021